Praise for

Fallen

One thing I loved about Detroit was the story line. It was great. The back story was well thought out and the characters were good. I enjoyed the story so much I immediately started reading the second one.
~ *Erzabet Enchantments*

In Reno the dream scenes were smokin hot and I loved them. It paved the way for Abby to lust after William so he could keep her safe from the demons chasing her through a rabid customer at the casino where she works. Great action, hot sex scenes and more celestial chess playing made this a good read. Looking forward to the next book in the series!
~ *Erzabet Enchantments*

FALLEN
Volume One

Detroit

Reno

TIFFANY AARON

Fallen Volume One
ISBN # 978-1-78184-661-2
©Copyright Tiffany Aaron 2013
Cover Art by Posh Gosh ©Copyright 2013
Interior text design by Claire Siemaszkiewicz
Totally Bound Publishing

Published in 2013 by Totally Bound Publishing, Newland House, The Point, Weaver Road, Lincoln, LN6 3QN, United Kingdom.

Totally Bound Publishing is an imprint of Total-E-Ntwined Limited.

DETROIT

Dedication

To everyone, who once long ago, read my Fallen books and loved my angels. Thank you, and I hope you realise that everyone deserves a second chance.

Chapter One

Celeste stared at the skyline of Detroit. She was bone-tired. *When is the torment going to end?* She didn't expect an answer, since God had turned His back on her a long, long time ago. The moment she had chosen to forsake Heaven and rebel against Him, she'd condemned herself to living without His touch in her life.

Just once, she thought, leaning her head against the window, she'd like to know there was someone out there thinking about her. Tapping her forehead against the glass, she grimaced, knowing it would never happen.

She brought her thoughts back to the problem facing her. For two weeks, a cunning hunter had stalked the city of Detroit, preying on young women. A third body had been found twenty-four hours ago, and while the police had searched for clues, none had been found. They were now desperate to find something that would reveal who the killer was. Celeste knew who had committed the crimes. Tomas was the reason she had moved to Detroit ten years ago.

At that time she had tried to connect with him, but the fallen angel had become wary through the centuries, and had learnt ways to hide from humans and Enforcers alike. Now, he was finally beginning his game, a game she hoped to stop before he killed more girls.

Stalking into the office, one of her best agents growled, "It's like he fucking vanished, Celeste. Not one damn clue." Al Risen slumped in his chair and glared at her. He had joined Celeste's investigation and security business seven years ago. With his expertise, the company had become known for getting the impossible done and keeping order in the Motor City.

"Of course he vanished." She didn't turn to look at him. "We have a serial killer on our hands."

Al groaned. "Do we have to deal with him?"

"You don't. I will."

"Hell, Montgomery has been trying to fuck you for months now. You're playing right into his fantasies, Celeste. How do we know he isn't committing these murders?"

"Why would he, Al? So I would have to beg for help?" Celeste laughed. "He doesn't want me that badly."

Al snorted. "Honey, he would do anything to have you. Trust me. I've seen it in his eyes."

Celeste had met Adam Montgomery at the Mayor's office several months ago. Before even walking into the office she had smelt the musky scent of leather, power and man. Her skin had flushed and she had felt her pussy become wet. Then she'd seen him standing by the desk.

Adam was taller than she was. He was broad shouldered and lean-hipped with skin tanned from hours spent in the sun. His unique light green eyes had focused on her. His lips were thin and slightly cruel. His light brown hair, streaked with golden highlights, barely brushed his shoulders. He'd worn his three-piece dark blue suit like he had been raised with money instead of on the streets, as rumoured.

She'd clenched her thighs and the throbbing in her clit had increased as her jeans rubbed against it. She'd tried to stay calm, but she hadn't been able to control her body's reaction. Her breasts had grown heavy and her nipples tightened to little pebbles. Celeste had never been so aroused, not even after an hour of foreplay, and Adam had known it. She had seen his own arousal flare in his eyes. The instant attraction had scared her.

He had asked her out that day and she had turned him down. No matter how many times he had asked since, she had said no. There was a danger in lusting after him. Celeste feared if she were to share his bed, she would lose her heart and she couldn't afford to lose any more of it.

Celeste put the memory away when Al cleared his throat. She said softly, "I've already set up a meeting."

"I'll go with you."

Celeste shook her head. "I have to go alone, Al. There have been three women killed. I'm willing to do whatever I have to do to catch him." Celeste pulled her coat on and walked from the office.

"Even play the whore for a demon." She overheard Al say as she left.

As Celeste walked to her car, she reviewed all the information she had found on Adam Montgomery. It didn't hurt to know everything she could about the man who was going to be her partner on this case.

Adam Montgomery was the leader of the Demons, a mortal gang that owned the Detroit streets. The Demons knew everything happening in the city, crime related or not, and they had a hand in almost every crime. Celeste had heard the rumours that there were some things Adam wouldn't allow in his city. Some crimes were too terrible for even Adam to contemplate.

Adam controlled most of Detroit by virtue of the fear that the Demons inspired. Unfortunately—or maybe fortunately—Adam didn't know the extent of the evil lurking in the shadows of the city. She did and it scared her.

* * * *

Adam stared at the tall blonde waiting for him at the bar. Damn, she was gorgeous. At almost six feet tall, she was still a few inches shorter than he was. She had curves in all the right places with a great set of tits and a long pair of legs. Her dark blonde hair was long, reaching the middle of her back in subtle waves. She had a heart-stopping face with full lips and a strong nose. She wore a 'don't mess with me' attitude like armour.

There was something about Celeste Young that made Adam think of diamonds. She was tough but brilliant, gleaming brightly in the dull world she occupied. Looking deep into her eyes, Adam could see there was an icy fire burning deep in her. Whether it was righteous anger or plain madness, he didn't want to know.

Every week for a month after he'd first met her, he had called her for a date. He wasn't used to being rejected. On the rare occasions when a woman said no, he would back off and move on to the next, but there was something about Celeste that haunted him. She was never far from his thoughts.

When he'd realised his fascination with the leggy blonde wasn't going away, he'd had Jakar, his assistant, look into her past. Oddly enough, it seemed she hadn't existed before she'd showed up in Detroit ten years ago. Her business had opened up one day in an office building downtown. Before that day, Jakar couldn't find anything. His right hand man thought he was an idiot to chase after a woman who didn't want him, but the mystery surrounding her drew him like a moth to a flame. Finally tired of getting turned down, he'd told her to call him when she was ready.

He knew why she'd called him. While he was excited to be getting a taste of Celeste Young, he was raging about the killer. How could he have got into the city without Adam's knowledge? Even though he already had men out looking for the killer, he was willing to join forces with Celeste, if only to get her to finally go out with him.

His cock stood at painful attention and he grinned. He might be considered the spawn of the Devil, but he was going to get a taste of Heaven tonight.

"Celeste," he murmured in her ear as he came up behind her, then bent his neck to nuzzle her soft skin. "Even in a smoky bar, you manage to smell good." He pressed closer to her, grinding his erection against her jean-covered ass.

He knew she was trying as hard as she could to stop her body from relaxing. She rubbed herself hard against him.

He groaned softly. "Careful, baby. I'm riding a thin line right now."

"Don't call me baby. That's what you call a petite blonde chewing bubble gum. I'm not the cheerleader type." Celeste smiled.

"Thank God for that, Celeste. I don't want to clean gum off my cock."

Celeste laughed. "What makes you think my mouth will be getting anywhere near your cock?"

"Just call it a hunch." Adam backed off and grabbed her arm. "Let's get out of here. This isn't a safe place for you." He'd noticed the stares they were getting.

She turned on him. "I can take care of myself, Adam. I don't need some macho man protecting me. Besides, I have a friend." She tenderly stroked the 9mm Glock strapped to her side.

Adam's cock twitched. He hoped she'd caress him just as gently when it was his turn.

"Are we clear, Adam?" Her smirk told him she knew what she was doing to him.

He snapped out of his daydream as a bottle broke behind them. "Celeste, the only reason you're still standing and not spread out on the bar is because you're with me. Every person in this bar knows what will happen if they mess with what's mine."

"You're pretty possessive for a man who hasn't even fucked me yet."

"After I do, you won't want another man," Adam promised.

"And you won't want another woman." Celeste sauntered out of the bar.

"I'm betting on that, Celeste," Adam whispered under his breath as he followed her swaying hips out into the parking lot. He opened the door of his truck for her then watched as she climbed in. He went around to the driver's side before sliding in behind the wheel.

"Where are we going?" Celeste asked as Adam started his truck. After leaving the lot, he headed in the direction of his house.

"Somewhere we can talk." Adam stared out of the window for a moment before shooting a quick glance at Celeste. Her white T-shirt was tight enough for him to know she wasn't wearing a bra and her nipples were pebbled against the cotton material. Surrendering to the urge, he reached over and caught her left nipple between his thumb and forefinger, yet somehow he managed to keep his attention on the road. Squeezing and pulling on it, he listened to her gasp in surprise then moan in delight. His cock was growing. Good thing he was wearing loose pants or he would have burst the zipper by now. The sound of Handel's Hallelujah chorus interrupted the moment.

"That's mine," Celeste muttered as she reached for her phone.

Adam groaned.

"Yeah...what is it?" Celeste threw a smile at Adam. She must have heard the frustration in his groan. "Okay, where was it found?"

Adam glanced at her. He slowed and pulled into an empty parking lot. Putting the truck in park, he watched her.

"We'll be right there... Yeah, Montgomery's with me." Celeste hung up.

"Where?" he asked. He presumed another body had been found somewhere.

"A vacant lot just off Grand River Avenue. Al says the body's been there a while. So this isn't a fresh kill."

"This makes it the fourth one though," Adam commented as he pulled out onto the street again then headed in the direction of Grand River.

"Unfortunately it looks like he's been killing for longer than we thought."

They were silent, letting the hockey game on the radio fill the quiet.

Chapter Two

Celeste reached deep inside her well of power as they pulled up to the lot. Even though the body had been there for a while, she might still be able to get some trace on Tomas. A death this violent would leave some sort of mark on the energy around it for weeks afterwards.

Celeste moved towards the crowd of police officers. She knew the body hadn't been moved yet—the stench of decay filled the air. She swallowed hard, trying to beat down the overwhelming feeling of fear clinging to the air in the lot. She was at full strength and she was getting the residue from the victim's last moments. The sensation in her chest warned her that she was going to find a message here.

The officers parted for her. Most of them had at some point worked with Celeste on various cases. She kept her eyes on the corpse on the ground, ignoring the police around her. The cross burned into the woman's chest ensured that Celeste would recognise the killer. She waved to the coroner to come and bag the body. She had seen all she needed.

"Who could do this?" Adam's face was contorted with disgust. He was breathing though his mouth, probably trying not to get sick from the smell.

"His name is Tomas. I've been following him for years now. I've always known he was capable of this, but until these, he's never killed. I wonder what made him decide to start?" Celeste stared into the shadows surrounding them.

Surprise tainted Adam's voice. "You know him?"

Celeste nodded. She was tuning into an angry feeling coming from the farthest corner of the lot. She headed in that direction. "Tomas has been moving about the country for years, never stopping anywhere for very long. I've been keeping tabs on him for a while. He came to Detroit about ten years ago and seemed to make it a permanent stop. I came here, set up shop and kept an eye on him. Now, he's starting to kill and it will only get worse from here on."

Holding up her hand, she stopped Adam's next question. She closed her eyes and connected with the tendrils of anger she felt vibrating in the air. The vision taking over her mind made her chest feel like it was going to burst into flame.

A woman knelt in front of Celeste. She was naked and begging for mercy. Celeste felt fierce pleasure swamping the man whose eyes she looked out of. He was enjoying the woman's fear. Like a rabid dog, he fell upon the woman. While the blood flowed, the woman's cries became weaker and Tomas' pleasure soared into ecstasy. Celeste wanted to pull out of the vision, but she knew she had to see it to the end. There might be some clue to Tomas' whereabouts.

As Tomas burnt the brand into the woman's chest, Celeste felt him focusing inside himself. There was the lightest touch on her mind. Tomas had known she would try to use the emotion around the woman's death to connect with him. She felt his triumph and his taunting of her. For some reason, Tomas had always felt she was the only Enforcer who could compete with him. In the end, that was all this was to Tomas—a competition to see who was smarter. Celeste heard his voice say, *"That's the first."*

A touch on her shoulder pulled her out of the vision. She turned to see Adam staring at her, worry shading his green eyes. He started to say something, but she shook her head. She didn't want to talk here, where the woman's fear still threatened to overwhelm her. She couldn't take the chance of being pulled under by the pain. It could destroy her.

"Where do we go now?" Adam asked as they climbed into his truck.

"Take me home. There isn't anything we can do tonight. She's been dead a while. The body won't give the police a lot of clues. We just have to hope that the people she was last with will know something."

"But you doubt it. Who is this Tomas?"

"A killer you don't want to tangle with, Adam. He is highly intelligent and he has abilities no one here has ever seen." Celeste didn't think Adam was ready to hear the truth about Tomas.

"What about our talk? You wanted to discuss something with me tonight." The gleam in Adam's eyes told Celeste he had figured out what she wanted.

She looked out of her window. Focusing on the homeless people dotting the sidewalk, she managed to get her lust under control. "Yes, we do have something to discuss, but not tonight. Things have changed. I need to rethink my plans."

Disappointment filled his eyes for a moment before he wiped them blank. He obviously didn't want her to know how much he'd been looking forward to their talk.

* * * *

She shut her door before Adam drove off. Sighing, Celeste walked through the darkness to her bedroom. She stripped her clothes off, then started the water for a bath, lighting the candles lining every space in her bathroom with a wave of her hand. The cleansing scent of cinnamon filled the air as she tried to forget about the vision, but she knew it wouldn't leave her mind anytime soon. She wouldn't be getting much sleep until the case was solved.

Sliding into the warm water, she leaned her head back. The flickering flames of the candles teased her mind. She saw shapes in the shadows. But were they the shades of the victims or the hints of ghosts to come? The only one who could have answered was lost to her.

Laughing ruefully, she admitted her rebellion had been the worst idea in her entire life. What had possessed her to turn her back on the very person who had created her? Lucifer's voice had been so tempting and she had been so gullible. It was only after her banishment that she had realised what he had cost her. Others had figured it out as well. They had begged God to let them come back, but He had turned away as surely as they had turned from Him.

The water cooled as she tried to remember what Heaven looked like. It wouldn't appear in her mind anymore, the memory having been wiped clean by her turning away. Being a fallen angel wasn't what Lucifer had claimed it would be. She had powers beyond mortal reckoning, but she was alone in the world. For an angel, being banished from the mind of God was a horrible thing. It felt like death, even though it took a lot for angels to die. It was even worse now that she was an Enforcer. She had to hunt down the fallen who preyed upon the mortals.

She stood in front of the mirror. Wiping the mist from the glass, she stared at the scar on her chest above her left breast. It was a cross. The fallen called it the mark of Cain. Every Enforcer wore one. Mika'il, the Captain of the Host, had burnt it into her flesh when she'd chosen to hunt her own kind.

Tomas was one of the fallen whose mind had slipped into the black abyss where his madness had taken control. He would kill until she stopped him. Since she wouldn't be getting help from Heaven or the Host, she would have to look to the mortal world. Adam Montgomery was her only choice. He had the power and the men to search the city, street by street if need be.

She remembered how quickly the lust had overcome her. That lust would be a useful thing for her. Unlike Tomas, who gained his power from fear and pain, Celeste and the other Enforcers gained their power from sex. Maybe God had given that power to the Enforcers to make up for their bleak existence. Maybe her power was a sign that God hadn't totally forsaken her.

Her heart had reacted to Adam as well. She was afraid she was only a few steps away from love. If she spent time with him, she could lose her heart. It wouldn't be the first time. Over the centuries, she had loved many mortals and she had cried every time one died. She could still feel the pain their death had caused her and she wasn't sure she could deal with more pain. She often wondered if her loving mortals was another way of God punishing her, yet she couldn't see Him using love as punishment.

Each day she felt herself crawling closer to the abyss. She didn't want to turn into one of the creatures she hunted. She had vowed to herself to end her existence before that happened. One more lover's death might just be too much for her.

The last victim's face flashed in the mirror. She saw the horror and the fear. Though she'd tracked many fallen angels though a hundred cities, Celeste knew that Adam might be the key to helping her find Tomas in Detroit. How many more would die if she didn't use Adam? She was afraid she knew the answer. Tomas would never stop on his own, so it was up to her to end his reign of terror. The risk to her heart and sanity were unimportant in view of the number of women Tomas could kill.

Her decision made, Celeste climbed into bed and whispered a quiet prayer. Old habits died hard.

Chapter Three

Adam studied the group of men gathered around the table. They were his top lieutenants in the Demons. These were some of the most feared men on the streets, ruling with an iron fist and swift judgement. The only thing these men understood was strength. Adam had proven his ruthlessness. His punishments were severe when his rules weren't followed — because of this, his men respected and feared him.

Adam had created his own mythology. He made sure his background stayed a mystery. He had appeared on the streets at the age of twelve and not even the best investigators could find anything out about him. He spread the rumours that he would kill anyone who asked about his past. Whether he really would or not, after one look in his green eyes, the rumours were believed. If there were any compassion or love in Adam's heart, he had hidden it deep. To be in control of everything around him, he knew he had to be cruel.

"Thanks for coming, gentlemen. I'm sure you have all heard about the killer hunting in our streets."

The grumbling among his men made it clear they weren't happy with the deaths. One of the first rules Adam had imposed when he'd become leader was no women or children were to be harmed. He remembered how helpless he had been when he was younger and he never wanted to cause such feelings in any child. So this Tomas had signed his own death warrant when he'd started killing women on Adam's territory.

"They've found a fourth body. She looks to be the first one he killed. Now, I need you to talk to your men. Get them out on the street. They need to find out anything they can on this guy. Find the places the homeless people are avoiding. It's usually the street people who know things before we do. Jakar will get you the information about where the bodies were found and who they were." Adam clenched his fists. "If something isn't done soon, we'll be seeing more dead women. I don't like dead women on my turf. It upsets me."

They nodded—they had seen what happened when Adam got upset. He brought the meeting to an end. As he walked into his office, he saw Jakar standing next to his desk. Adam could never remember if he had found Jakar or if the strange man had found him. His right hand man was tall and thin with amber-coloured eyes that seemed to glow red at times. Jakar had an answer for every question Adam might ask. Or if he didn't have the answer, he would find it. Adam had never asked Jakar where he got the information—he wasn't sure he wanted to know.

"What have you got, Jakar?" Adam asked as he sat down. There were papers piled in neat stacks everywhere on his desk.

"The Russians have called. They would like to meet with you as soon as possible. They have been approached by an outside source trying to get them to deal with him. He seems to think he can get them better rates."

"It's good to know the Russians are willing to talk to me first before going with this guy."

Jakar shrugged. "After you saved his son, the Russian boss is willing to repay you with this courtesy. Also, I'm sure he knows you own the whole city. Nothing coming or going escapes your attention. So, it pays to be on your good side."

"True. Set up an appointment with them as soon as possible. I don't want this to get out of hand. What else?"

"Celeste Young has called for you." Disapproval dripped from Jakar's voice.

"You don't approve of the lady. Why not?" Adam was amused. Jakar had never made his feelings known about any of the other women Adam had dated.

"She's a distraction you don't need right now, Montgomery. She will take your attention away from your business."

"Not all women are distractions. You've never said anything about the others." Adam started reading the papers he had to sign.

"That's true. But none of the bimbos you dated before could have occupied you for more than a week or so. Celeste will demand more from you."

Adam glanced up. "Do you know her?"

The evasive look shooting through Jakar's eyes told Adam his friend was about to lie to him. "Only what I found out while I investigated her for you. I don't trust a woman who seems to have appeared out of nowhere."

"Liar." Adam stopped Jakar's protest. "I don't care. Now, take these papers and get them filed. I'll deal with Celeste."

"Fine." Jakar stalked out of the office.

Adam laughed, knowing Jakar hated it when Adam didn't take his advice. He dialled Celeste's cell number from memory. Leaning back in his chair, he waited to hear her sultry voice.

"Hello?"

"Hey there, angel."

A shocked silence followed his greeting. Was she surprised that he'd called?

"Hello, Montgomery. We need to finish the discussion we started."

"Started? We didn't even get to think about it." He licked his lips.

"I've thought about our arrangement. Now we need to talk." Celeste's voice held a hint of uncertainty.

"Are you sure about this, Celeste? I know what you're going to ask for. You know what my price will be."

She sighed. "I really have no choice, Adam. You're the only one with the resources to help me. I'll pay your price without regret if this helps me catch Tomas."

"My place or yours?"

"We'll meet somewhere neutral first."

"Sure. I own a restaurant on Woodward. It's a couple blocks down from the Fox. I can pick you up."

"No, I'll meet you there about seven. It's going to be hard driving downtown tonight. The Wings are playing at home again."

"At seven," Adam agreed and hung up. "Jakar," he called as he walked out of his office.

"No need to bellow, Montgomery. I'm right here." Jakar came up to him.

"Make sure there are a dozen red roses and a bottle of champagne chilling at my house around ten."

Adam could have sworn he heard Jakar hiss as the man turned to glare at him. "You're bringing her home tonight?"

Adam nodded. "She might as well start paying for my services tonight. Don't worry, old man. She won't be staying around long after the killer's caught." He reached out to pat Jakar's shoulder.

Jakar dodged his hand. "I'll have everything ready, but don't expect me to like it."

"That's fine. You're not the one who's going to be fucking her tonight." Adam walked out of the door, ignoring Jakar's shiver of fear and disgust.

* * * *

Adam was glad he had a napkin. It was useful to wipe the drool from his chin. He had never found a woman more attractive than Celeste.

Her blonde hair was pulled up in a complex knot with tendrils of curls lying on her neck and forehead. Her body was lovingly encased in a sky blue silk sheath that matched her eyes, covering her to the neck in front then plunging deep in the back, exposing her creamy skin to his heated gaze. It was obvious Celeste had decided to get the payment over with. Little did she know that it wasn't going to be a one-night pay-out.

"I've got all my guys out looking for witnesses. They'll scour all the areas where the bodies were found and talk to the people who won't say a word to the police. If he can be found by sheer manpower, we'll get him." Adam sipped from his crystal wineglass.

Celeste's gaze slid over his face. He wondered if she saw the lust burning in his eyes. He would have thought she would be nervous about the upcoming change in their relationship, considering how hard she had fought it before. But when he looked at her, he didn't see nervousness. He saw a rather weary acceptance on her face, as if she had always known this was going to happen.

He leaned over and covered her hand with his. "You know what my price is, Celeste. What made you decide to pay it?"

"As I said, I have no other choice. There is no one else who can help me find Tomas. So, I'll use the best I have available to me. Being the crime boss of Detroit, you have avenues open to you that I don't. Even though you are a criminal and a ruthless businessman, I know when you give me your word, you'll keep it."

"Honour among thieves then, Celeste."

She shrugged and looked away. "Honour among the fallen, I think is a better term for it."

Puzzled by her cryptic statement, he filed it away to think on later. "I want you to know that you will be my lover for the duration of the case. This isn't a one night thing, Celeste. Until we put Tomas behind bars, you're mine."

Again, Celeste didn't look surprised. "From the moment I met you, I knew we couldn't have just one night together. Until the end of the case, you are mine. I don't share either."

He acknowledged her right to make that demand as he stood and led her outside to where a sleek black limo was waiting.

"Trying to make a good impression, Adam?" she asked as she slid in.

Adam climbed in after her. "I don't want to be distracted by driving tonight. I want it to be a memorable night. If we ended up dead, it would put a damper on the evening."

"Ending up dead is the least of my worries," Celeste mumbled.

Adam pulled her close. He didn't want to talk anymore. After pressing his lips against hers, he nibbled gently. She moaned quietly, then opened her mouth to allow his tongue in. Stroking in and out, he imitated the more intimate act. He slid his hand down her shoulder to cup her full breast in his hand, and fondled her nipple roughly.

"Adam," Celeste begged. "Harder."

Adam took his hand away. "Unfasten the dress, Celeste," he ordered.

She reached up and unclasped the button at her neck holding the dress on. It fell down to her waist to reveal her tits. He stared. They were beautiful—creamy mounds tipped by dark pink nipples. They would be a handful. He reached out one finger and flicked one bud. She jumped and, liking her response, he flicked it again to see if she'd do the same.

"It's like there's an electric current running from your tits to your cunt," he commented.

Celeste nodded. His face flushed. He felt sweat building on his forehead. She was the most responsive woman he had ever had.

Pinching her nipple tight between his fingers, he twisted slightly. Celeste cried out softly.

"You said harder, Celeste." He took both breasts in his hands. Kneading them firmly, he pulled and tugged at her nipples.

"More," she pleaded.

Adam licked his fingertips. When they were wet, he captured her tits again, and the touch of his damp, warm fingers caused Celeste to gasp. The more he pinched, the hotter she got. Suddenly, she threw back her head, arched her back and screamed.

Shit! Adam had never had a woman climax just from his hands on her tits. He gentled his touch to ease her. He felt the wetness of pre-cum warm the head of his cock. He needed to get her back to his house so he could finally fuck her like he'd been dreaming about for years.

"Was that good for you, darling?" Adam asked quietly after a few minutes.

Celeste rolled her eyes at him. "You have to ask? I'm embarrassed. I've never had that happen before." She blushed.

"Never?" Adam was slightly amazed. Then he sent her a grin. "Obviously you just needed the right hands for the job." He jumped slightly when Celeste's hand grazed the front of his pants.

She winked at him. "Maybe you should get us home. I don't think once will be enough, especially since I can't wait to get this huge cock inside me."

Hell! If she kept teasing him, he would never make it to his place. Celeste skipped her fingers up and down the length of his dick.

"Spread your legs a little wider," Celeste demanded while sucking on Adam's ear lobe.

He spread them. She slid her hand down and firmly gripped his balls. His heart raced and he knew she revelled in the power she had over him.

"Suck in your stomach a little."

Adam did with a small moan. He knew what was next. She undid his belt, unbuttoned his slacks and eased the zipper down over his raging hard-on. Celeste pushed the front of his briefs down until his cock sprang out. She purred in appreciation. Taking him roughly in her hand, she started stroking. Sliding her other hand to his balls, she fondled and squeezed him.

"You feel so good. I'm wet thinking about this wonderful cock pounding into me. I want to feel your balls brushing my thighs. I can't wait to feel your cum making me wet and sticky."

Slow and gentle, rough and fast, she played a tune on his cock that had never been played before. Her voice and tongue in his ear. To hell with control. Two hard pumps of her hand and he exploded.

Cum spurted out onto her hands and his pants and shirt. His hips kept jerking as she softly soothed his heated flesh. He finally came back to earth as the car slowed and made the turn into his driveway.

She fastened her dress as he stripped off his shirt. Wiping his pants, he shook his head at her. "I look like a fucking eighteen-year-old who just saw his first porn flick." Tossing her his shirt, he straightened and fastened his pants again. "Wipe your hands. We're at my place. You and I can't do anything about Tomas tonight. I've got my people working on it. Tomorrow will be soon enough. Get ready to enjoy the rest of the night."

Chapter Four

The limo stopped in front of Adam's house. The chauffeur opened the door and Celeste stepped out. Her power was back to full strength from the climaxes they had enjoyed in the limo. She smiled to herself. It was going to be a great night.

The front door swung open and a thin, dark man with strange, amber-coloured eyes stood aside and studied Celeste as they entered.

"Bringing home heavenly bodies, Montgomery?" he asked in a heavily accented voice.

"Yes. And she's mine, Jakar. Don't you or any of the others forget it," Adam growled as he continued up the curved staircase.

"How can we resist the light?" Jakar raked his stare over Celeste's body and shut the door. Turning back to the retreating couple, he said calmly, "Be wary of her, Montgomery. There is a darkness surrounding Miss Young that is making me uneasy."

What the hell is a true demon doing here? Celeste followed Adam to his room. As an Enforcer, Celeste should have been concerned with the fact that a true demon was settled in Detroit, but she found she could only deal with one problem at a time and Jakar wasn't the worst threat.

To give her time to think, Celeste suggested that Adam take a shower. After throwing his clothes on the nearest chair, he headed for the bathroom. Celeste stripped and curled up in his bed. She closed her eyes as she thought about the man whose very touch caused her to go up in flames.

Adam Montgomery had grown up on the streets of Detroit where he had learnt about life the hard way, and he still had the scars to prove it. Was there a way she could reach him beyond the walls he'd built around his heart and soul? She knew his feelings on relationships. She also knew he didn't understand the seriousness of them becoming involved. As she waited for him to get out of the shower, she fell asleep.

Celeste found herself standing over a woman. She watched as the woman writhed on the sheets and realised the sounds she was hearing were really moans of pain. Thin red welts were appearing across her chest and thighs. A handprint blossomed on her right cheek. Her legs were spreading apart slowly, as she fought someone Celeste could not see. With a scream of pleasure and pain, the woman arched her back, but only for a few seconds. Looking down Celeste was appalled to see small cuts appear on the woman's breasts and bite marks on her thighs. She gagged as a cut raced across her throat.

Celeste turned to see the man who appeared, leaning over the woman. It was Tomas. She had somehow connected with him while he killed his latest victim. What could she learn while the woman endured the last moments of her life? The room was dirty. It had the feel of age and abandonment. There were some city sounds coming from outside, but she could tell it wasn't a busy section of the city.

She didn't hear Jakar enter the room until the true demon hissed. She had been engrossed in trying to find Tomas' hiding place. Coming out of the dream, Celeste noticed Adam standing just inside the room with a towel hanging from his hand. After grabbing the forgotten towel in Adam's hand, Jakar wrapped it around her throat.

"Doc is downstairs. Go get him. She needs medical care."

Stunned, Adam stood still. He was staring at the wounds covering her body.

"Montgomery, go." Jakar's harsh voice jolted Adam out of his trance. Together, Jakar and Celeste watched Adam race from the room. Jakar stared down at Celeste. His amber eyes gleamed in the lamplight. "Miss Young, it seems you have bewitched my boss. Is it a good or a bad thing? I don't know." His hand flexed on the towel. "It would be so easy to get rid of you while you are weak. Montgomery can't afford a distraction right now."

Celeste's eyes narrowed. Jakar found himself flung across the room, then slammed against the wall. He stood pinned to the wall. Celeste's gaze never left his.

"Don't ever think I'll be weak enough for you to kill me. What is a true demon doing here?"

Jakar didn't struggle. He watched as the cuts slowly healed and the welts disappeared. "What is one of the Enforcers doing in Detroit fucking my life up?"

"I am here for the killer, Jakar. Not to mess with you or your life. I wouldn't think you could manipulate Adam Montgomery."

"I'm not doing anything to him. He's too strong. He's already achieving a goal we've been working towards." Jakar was smug.

"Goal? What are you trying to achieve?"

"Someone, whether good, evil or a mix of both, had to bring this city under control. You know what happens when there is no balance."

Celeste did know. The Host was sent down to restore it by any way necessary. There were no boundaries set, no rules made. The Host would be brutal and thorough. Death to all until nature was right again.

"Will you tell him what you are?" Jakar felt the need to ask.

She studied Jakar with narrowed eyes. "I will if he asks. But will he believe me?"

Jakar shrugged.

She sat up in the middle of Adam's bed. She pulled the red silk sheet up to her waist. Taking her eyes off Jakar, she turned towards the door. Jakar relaxed and moved closer to her. He may have been a true demon, but Celeste was an Enforcer with more power in her fingertips than he had in his entire body.

Adam burst into the room followed by Doc. When he had left, Celeste had been covered with welts and bleeding from a slash to the throat. There she sat, her wounds healed. Jakar was sitting warily at the end of the bed.

"Where's the woman, Montgomery?" Doc growled. He was holding a black medical bag in his hand.

"She's on the bed, Doc. Guess she isn't as badly hurt as I thought." Adam was puzzled. He stared at Celeste who gave him a slow smile.

"We'll be heading back to bed, Doc. Montgomery will sort it out." Jakar started to pull Doc from the room. Stopping, he bowed slightly to Celeste before he left.

Adam was amazed. Had he imagined everything? He could have sworn Celeste's throat was slashed. He scrubbed his hand over his face. Celeste watched him with a strange look in her eyes.

She waved him to the side of the bed. As he moved closer, she climbed to her hands and knees and prowled forward. He caught a glimpse of a tattoo on her back, but before he could ask her about it, she caught hold of his semi-erect dick. She stroked it once. As their eyes connected, she bent her head and ran her tongue from the base of his shaft to the head. He groaned, and any worry about her injuries slid from his mind as she licked him.

Eagerly, Celeste swallowed Adam's long, thick shaft. She sucked the drops of pre-cum from the slit while she grabbed his balls to roll them roughly in her hand. He twisted his hand in her hair and was soon hammering his cock into her mouth.

Her mouth felt like he imagined her cunt would — hot and moist. As he retreated, she tightened her lips around him and sucked hard. When he thrust back in, she relaxed her throat and took him all in. Throwing back his head, Adam moaned and his hoarse cries filled the room. Adam felt her fingers slide down to the smooth piece of skin right behind his balls. With a few more of her deft touches, he exploded, spilling hot cum into her throat.

She sucked him dry. When his hips had stopped jerking, she slipped her mouth away. Smiling, Celeste helped him climb into bed. He lay on his back as his breathing slowed. Curling up beside him, she ran her fingers up and down his chest.

His cock hardened again, and he trailed his hands over her body. Celeste skipped her thumb over the ruddy head and laughed.

"You still have some life."

"Wait and see."

Adam rolled her onto her back, then kissed and licked his way down from her ears to her breasts. He paused to stare at the cross-shaped scar that marred one otherwise perfect globe. It wasn't the time to talk about it though. Pinching one nipple, he took the other deep into his mouth. He sucked and bit until she couldn't stay still. She cried out as he moved his mouth to the other one. He continued to ply the wet nipple with his fingers. He could feel her orgasm building. He left her breasts right before she came.

Running his tongue down to her belly button, he was surprised to encounter a butterfly shaped jewel piercing it. He circled the jewel with his tongue, distracting her as he trailed his fingers up her thighs.

"Spread your legs, darling," he ordered softly. He rose to his knees and stared down at her pussy. It was clean-shaven except for a small patch of light gold curls. Using his fingers, he gently parted her wet lips to see the hard little button they hid. He leant down and breathed in deeply. She smelt wonderful. While he looked at her, she became wet with the glistening juices from her pussy.

"Celeste, you're beautiful. Your cunt's all wet and hot. Your clit is begging me to taste it. You've tasted me, darling. Now it's my turn."

Celeste pushed herself up on her elbows to watch him stretch out on his stomach. She gave a little cry as he took one long swipe along her cunt. He settled in to feast on her hard clit with teeth, tongue and lips. He slid a finger into her clinging pussy. Starting a slow pace, he pressed one, then two fingers, in and out.

The combination of his tongue stroking her clit and his fingers thrusting in and out of her pussy seemed to light a fire in her. Celeste's hips were bucking in rhythm to Adam's fingers. She pleaded with him to finish it. He smiled.

Adam covered his thumb in her cream. Then he bore down on her clit with his mouth, her pussy with his fingers and her ass with his thumb. When he breached her barrier with his thumb and sank into her tight hole, she screamed and grabbed his hair. Pressing his head to her lifted pussy, she came hard.

Before the waves slowed, Adam pulled away then grabbed a condom from the stash he kept on the shelf of his headboard. After rolling one over his cock, he draped her thighs over his forearms and thrust hard into her. Her contractions drove him into his own mind-shattering climax, his hot cum flooding the rubber in spurts. He threw back his head and yelled.

"Great distraction, Celeste," Adam commented after he caught his breath.

Celeste rose up on her side to look down at him as he lay beside her. "What makes you think I was trying to distract you? I thought you would enjoy it."

"I did enjoy it. Hell, I think I lost my mind there at the end. But did you think the sex would make me forget about what happened tonight?" Adam scrubbed his hands over his face, then took care of the used condom. "What the hell did happen, Celeste?"

Celeste sighed. Pushing her hair from her face, she climbed out of bed. Adam watched her wander over to the large window and pull the curtains open. The moonlight pouring in highlighted the tattoo he had noticed earlier. An angel holding aloft a flaming sword marked her lower back. He joined her at the window and lightly touched her skin above the tattoo.

"What does the angel represent?" Adam asked quietly.

"It is the Archangel Mika'il."

"He's the warrior angel, right?" Adam didn't know much about angels.

"Yes. He guards my back for me. He also reminds me I can't go back."

"Back where?"

"Home." Celeste turned to face Adam. The light bathed her body in silver.

He gently touched the vicious cross-shaped scar marring her left breast. "I noticed this before. Where did you get it?"

She stared over his shoulder into the dark. Her thoughts seemed to be far away.

"What happened earlier, Celeste? What kind of dream was that?"

Her eyes refocused on him. "It wasn't a dream, Adam. Somewhere, Tomas left us another body tonight."

Adam looked puzzled. "Are you telling me you're psychic?"

"I'm linked with him, Adam."

"If you know who he is, why don't you go and get him?"

Shaking her head, Celeste turned back to the window. "I know who he is, but his whereabouts are unclear to me. I'm only linked to him because we are brethren."

"What are you talking about?"

"It's a long story. Centuries old and hidden from mortals."

"Mortals?"

"Couldn't this wait? I'm sure we could find something better to do with our mouths."

"No, this can't wait, Celeste. Who are you?" Staring at the woman he had just had the most incredible sex of his life with, Adam sat down on the edge of the bed.

She laughed softly. "It's a long story that started before humans were even created. He made us to adore and worship Him. Free will wasn't really in our vocabulary."

"Us? Our?"

"Angels."

"So you're telling me you're an angel? I fucked an angel?" Adam was incredulous. How could such a beautiful, seemingly intelligent woman believe she was an angel? She was crazy.

There was sadness in Celeste's laugh. "At one time, I was an angel. I was happy. Then seeds of discontent were sown. He had created humans, and He loved you. I became jealous and when Lucifer rose up in rebellion against Him, I was swept up. By the time the dust had cleared, I was banished from Heaven and forced to endure life on earth."

Adam heard despair tinge Celeste's voice. "What are you?"

"I'm one of the fallen. Those angels banished with Lucifer for our rebellion. That's why I have the tattoo. It's to remind me that like Adam and Eve, I too am barred from my Garden of Eden."

"What about the scar?"

"There are some of us who have repented. We would love to go home if we were ever allowed to. Because of that and because we hunt down those of our brethren who prey on humans, we are branded with a cross. Our brethren call it the mark of Cain."

"Cain? Didn't Cain murder his brother?"

"That is what they think we are doing. We are choosing to serve out our banishment in a less evil way. We are known as the Enforcers."

"But isn't sex against the rules or something for angels?"

"Maybe if I was a true angel, Adam, but God allows the Fallen this one joy."

Adam was having a hard time with the thought of her being any kind of angel.

"Why don't we rest now? Things will be different in the morning." Her voice was soothing.

Adam found himself lying back and falling asleep even though he wanted to talk. "Why will it be different?"

"Because I won't be here." Was what he heard as he drifted to sleep.

* * * *

Meanwhile in Reno, Nevada

William Bradford was startled awake as his covers were jerked off and the cold air rushed over his body.

"Damn!" William shot straight up.

"Watch your mouth, Enforcer." The harsh voice warned him the intruder in his room wasn't a person he wanted to mess with.

Climbing out of bed, he pulled on the faded jeans he had thrown on the chair the night before. He ran his hand through his hair as he stalked past his night visitor. He didn't really want to talk to Mika'il. The self-righteous prick really got on his nerves.

William stalked into the living room while Mika'il followed leisurely behind him.

"What are you doing here?" William asked. He stood at the window, looking out over the lights of Reno.

"If you had been paying attention to your dreams, you would know why I'm here," Mika'il complained.

"I'm no longer one of yours, sir. The dreams would have driven me insane long ago if I paid any attention to them." William was respectful. Even though he didn't like the angel, he knew it wouldn't pay to make him mad.

"One of your fellow Enforcers is having a bit of a problem. You should think about heading out to see her."

"Celeste." William turned to look at Mika'il. "Why do you care? In all the centuries since our banishment, you have never gone out of your way to help us."

Mika'il stared over William's shoulder into the world outside the window. "I've done what I have been allowed to do. You haven't made it easy on me. Who do you think sends you the dreams?"

"Someone who wishes to drive us crazy. Have you any idea what they do to us?"

The archangel shrugged. William knew Mika'il wasn't unsympathetic to the fallen, but he had reached his limit of patience with their whining long ago. "Deal with them, William. They are part of your punishment. Maybe if you had thought about everything before you rebelled, you wouldn't be in this position."

William smirked. "That's me. I've always raced in where angels feared to tread, sir."

Mika'il smiled slightly. William had often made Mika'il laugh, even during the worst moments. "That's true, William. I need you to go to Detroit. Celeste needs help. You are the only one she trusts."

"Why are you here? The head of His Host of Heaven shouldn't be concerned with a fallen."

"We all have our weaknesses and it looks like mine might be your kind." Mika'il looked at him. "Just go to Celeste, William." He disappeared before William could say yes or no.

"Damn angel. Coming and going like he owns the place. I guess I'm heading for the Motor City."

Chapter Five

Jakar stood in the shadows away from the pale, early morning sunlight, and stared at Adam lying in bed. As if sensing Jakar's presence, Adam woke quickly.

"What is it, Jakar? Where's Celeste?"

At Celeste's name, fear flared in Jakar. He didn't trust the Enforcer, even though he knew he wasn't her number one concern at the moment. "Celeste left earlier this morning."

"She left? Where did she go?"

Shrugging, he watched Adam climb from the bed before saying, "You need to be careful getting involved with her, Adam. She isn't like you."

"So she told me. I'd never have thought someone who looks like she does would be crazy."

"Crazy?"

"What am I supposed to think about her? She tells me she's a fallen angel. Get real, Jakar."

"What if I told you it's true? Celeste Young really is one of the fallen, Montgomery. She has lived for centuries. Since she can never return to Heaven, she searches out the evil haunting the world. How would you handle that?"

"I can tell she makes you nervous." Adam pulled on his robe, and the worried glance he shot Jakar told the demon his boss thought he might be losing touch with reality.

"Yes, she does."

"I never thought I'd see the day when you would be nervous about a woman." Adam laughed as he made his way to his bathroom.

"She could destroy me if she should choose to do so," Jakar stated softly.

Adam turned back. "Destroy you? How?"

"She has more power in her than I would ever dream of having. Even the fallen don't like my kind."

"What are you, a vampire?"

"No. The point is not what I am. The point is her agenda is not the same as yours. She doesn't care about the things you care about."

"I only fucked her. I'm not going to marry her." Adam went into the bathroom. A few seconds later, he stuck his head back out. "Get a hold of the guys. See if anyone has heard anything about this killer."

"Sure thing, boss." Jakar left, knowing that Adam was already doomed. You couldn't fuck an angel—even a fallen one—without falling in love. He went downstairs to do as he was ordered and to wait for Adam.

When Adam arrived at his office, Jakar was hanging up the phone.

"Has anyone found anything out?" Adam demanded.

Jakar shook his head. "They have some leads, but nothing's panned out yet."

"Keep me posted." Adam grabbed his cell phone and headed back out of the door.

"Where are you going?"

"To find our favourite angel and see what she can tell me."

Jakar wondered if he should just pack up and leave town. There were some fallen and Enforcers who would never allow a true demon to live, but Celeste had had the chance to kill him last night and she hadn't.

* * * *

"You spent the night with him," Al stated.

"Only part of the night." Celeste pulled her hair up in a ponytail.

"So he fucked you and then let you leave?" Al sounded sceptical.

"Why not?"

"From the way he's been panting after you, I'd have thought he'd tie you to his bed and keep you there for a couple weeks, at least."

"That's what I would have done if she had stuck around." Adam's voice sliced through the air.

They both whirled around to find Adam leaning in the office doorway. There was a look of anger in his green eyes that seemed to be warning Al about something, but Celeste wasn't sure what.

"Hey, Celeste, I'm going to follow up on that lead you gave me. Talk at you later." Al darted around Adam and jogged down the hall. He must have decided to get out before the fur flew, since Celeste could take care of herself.

"Not much of a knight in shining armour, is he?" Adam shut and locked the door.

Celeste turned to face him. She casually caressed him with her eyes. His T-shirt was red and lovingly showed off his broad shoulders and flat stomach. His faded jeans hugged his thighs and left no doubt in her mind that his cock, at least, was happy to see her. She motioned for him to turn around. Grinning, he did. The faded denim cupped his tight ass perfectly. She wanted him again. When he was facing her, she smiled.

"You outweigh Al by fifty pounds and you're taller than he is by five inches. Al might not stay to defend me, but he's got one thing going for him—he's smart. He might not save me, but he would never be in a situation where he would need to. He would have solved the problem before it ever got to that."

"So you value intelligence over brawn, huh?" Adam stalked her.

Celeste knew what he was doing. She was willing to allow him to capture her. "In most situations, being smart is better than being strong. I can take care of myself. I don't need anyone's help."

"Especially mine. You don't need my help because you're an angel." His voice was sarcastic. Adam pinned Celeste against her desk, pressing his hard body to hers. Her cheeks burned.

"Oh, I need your help with something." Ignoring the taunt, she slid her hands down to his hips then pulled him towards her, so his erection pushed against her mound. She rubbed her breasts on his chest.

"This probably isn't a good idea," Adam mumbled.

"This is always a good idea. Kiss me, damn you." Letting go of his hips, she locked her arms around his neck to bring his head down to hers.

In no time at all, she was naked and sprawled across her desk. Thank goodness he had remembered to lock the door. As he stared down at her tits, his mouth began to water. Slowly, almost hesitantly, he reached out to cup her right breast and squeezed. Celeste made an urgent noise in her throat.

"Do you want more, Celeste?"

She nodded. He palmed both of her plump breasts. Squeezing and kneading them, he studied her with narrowed eyes. He wondered what she was thinking. He found her hard nipples and tugged. Her back arched as she moaned softly. Leaning down, he took one into his mouth. He sucked hard, flicking the other with his fingers. He soon had her writhing on the desk.

"Adam, please."

"Please what, Celeste? Please touch your wet pussy? Please fuck your hot mouth with my cock? What do you want from me?"

"Everything. I want everything."

Adam trailed his fingers down her stomach, flirting with the jewel at her belly button. He slid his fingers between her wet lips and stroked as her thighs fell open to give him better access. Pinching her clit between his fingers, he bit down gently on her nipple.

She cried out as his lips left her body. Grabbing hold of her legs, he dragged her across her desk until her hips rested on the edge.

Her body jerked as his warm breath bathed her pussy. "Oh my."

"'Oh my' is right, sweetheart," Adam whispered right before he buried his face in her pussy.

Celeste seemed to come undone at the feel of his tongue plunging into her. Soon, he replaced his fingers with his tongue, working furiously as his mouth fastened on her clit. He bit it and flicked it hard with the tip of his tongue.

"Harder, Adam. Please," Celeste begged shamelessly.

Tearing himself away from her sweet pussy, Adam surged to his feet. Ripping open his jeans, he yanked out his cock then thrust into her hard again and again. The third time, he felt her pussy milk his cock mercilessly. He wasn't going to last long. Something about Celeste seemed to always have him hanging on the edge of pleasure.

Maybe it was the way she moved her body in rhythm with his. Maybe it was the way she allowed herself to give into the desire. Whatever it was, he went with it, not willing to give up what they had.

He saw her grip the edge of the desk as he slammed into her. He worried about hurting her for a fleeting moment, but realised if he was doing anything Celeste didn't like, she'd stop him. So he gave himself over to the sensations, and his balls tightened as his climax hit him.

Adam came, but managed to keep enough strength to make sure Celeste did as well. When she screamed his name as her orgasm swept through her, he knew he'd done his job.

He lay draped over her, recovering, as their breathing evened out. Groaning slightly, he slid from her then helped her stand. They cleaned up, and Adam winced as he realised he hadn't used a condom.

"Sorry about no protection. I got carried away."

She shrugged. "No big deal. I can't get pregnant or catch any human diseases, so you're safe."

Obviously her delusion of being an angel was more serious than he thought, but he wasn't willing to give her up yet.

"Don't ever leave me again, Celeste. I won't be quite as nice next time," Adam ordered.

She laughed and began dressing. "You're the only one who can leave, Adam? No woman should have the nerve to leave you. We're in trouble if you think I'll be listening to you now."

"Celeste," Adam warned as he zipped his jeans up.

"Don't take that tone, Adam. I've been around far longer than you."

Adam's phone rang before he could answer her. "Montgomery." He listened. "Okay, thanks, Jakar." He hung up and looked smugly at Celeste. "You don't need my help, huh?"

Celeste didn't answer him. After grabbing her Glock, she slipped on a jacket then headed out of the door.

"Where are you going?" Adam stalked after her.

"Another body's been found. We need to get there. The trail might lead us to Tomas."

"How did you know about the body? Did you get a call before I got here?"

Shaking her head, she got in her car. Looking at him, she quirked an eyebrow. "I didn't get a phone call. Are you coming?"

Adam noticed the bright red brand her low-cut shirt revealed. "Does it hurt?"

"Yes." She turned the key.

He ran around to slide in next to her. "Is Al going to meet us?"

"No."

He wondered about her short answers. "Isn't that the lead he was going to check out?"

"He was lying. He was leaving us alone. He probably went down to the coffee shop to flirt with the waiter."

Chapter Six

Adam was still mulling over the 'waiter' comment when Celeste pulled into an empty lot crawling with cops. They barely even acknowledged her as she strolled up to the body. Adam felt his stomach turn as they looked down at the woman.

Her body had been beaten and sliced. Thin cuts ran up and down her legs. There were bite marks on her breasts, but the fatal cut through the woman's throat was what shocked Adam the most. They were similar to the wounds Celeste had seemed to suffer last night. He shook his head as he remembered that those injuries had disappeared by the time he'd got back with the doctor. Could she really have been connected to the killer?

"Who is he?" Adam asked.

Celeste stared down at the body. She felt sorrow for a young life snuffed out too soon. "Tomas is one of the fallen. We are connected, but I'm only now beginning to pick up any sort of clues from him. Last night was the strongest one I've gotten so far." She headed back to her car.

The police officers ignored them since they were familiar with her being around. She was one of the good guys, but Adam was a wild card. He had his hand in most of the crime in Detroit, and it didn't pay to annoy someone as powerful as Montgomery.

"Where are we going?"

Celeste held in a small moan as she slid into the vehicle. The brand on her chest was burning. The pain radiated out through her nerves.

"Why do you search for me, sister?" The voice entered her mind harshly. She blinked and stared out through the windshield. Tomas stood on the other side of the lot. At least his image did. He was somewhere far from her reach.

A laugh echoed. *"Of course I'm not around here. I'm not going to make it easy for you to find me."*

"Why did you do this?" Celeste asked.

"You've never understood, my dear. Almost since the moment we were banished, you were looking for a way back. I did it because I can."

"This is cruel and wrong, Tomas."

"So was banishing us from Heaven, love. Here on earth, we are gods."

"You are playing at being Him, choosing life or death for your victims."

"It has never been that simple, Celeste."

"Celeste?" Adam touched her arm. She was staring out of the window. What was she thinking? Adam wanted to wrap his arms tightly around her. His body thought it was a good idea. No matter how strong she seemed on the outside, there was a fragile peace held inside her soul. He longed to get close and see if it would calm his heart.

All of his life, Adam had fought to survive. He had stayed away from using drugs because he saw how it ruined lives, but being the hypocrite he admittedly was, he'd sold them—it was the only way he'd been able to make a living. Slowly, he had made his way through the ranks of the criminal underworld. Then he'd been recruited into the Demons. When he'd become their leader, he'd turned the gang into a business. Soon, he'd had everything he wanted— money, power and respect. Who cared if the only reason he had any of it was because people feared him? It was better to have them fear him than to have any of them as friends.

Then Celeste had strolled into the mayor's office. His cock had taken notice of her firm tits and luscious ass right away. His mind had found an equal in the quickness of her wit and intelligence. His heart had fallen in love with all of those things, plus the gentleness of spirit hidden beneath the hard shell she presented to the world.

"Celeste?" he tried again.

Jerking, she looked at him. "What?"

"Where did you go?"

After turning on the car, she put it in drive. "What are you talking about?"

"One moment you were here. The next you're staring like a zombie out the window."

"I was thinking about something." Celeste pulled out onto Woodward Ave. She was heading towards the river where they'd found the body.

Adam's phone rang. "Montgomery."

"There was a hockey game last night," Jakar said.

"So?"

"The dead woman was seen at the game."

"Holy shit. Don't tell me one of the Red Wings is a serial killer?" Adam was appalled.

"No. I think he might pick them up at the games. I just finished talking to one of our contacts in the police department. Seems like the latest victim's friends reported her missing this morning. They saw her leave with a tall man who might have been blonde."

"Any other description?"

"That's all our contact could tell us right now. There didn't seem to be any kind of argument or anything. Nothing to draw attention to them. No one can give a good description of him."

"Damn! Keep our guys out looking. Someone had to have seen something." Adam hung up. He looked at Celeste. "He's picking them up at the Wings games. Weren't the other ones found the day after a hockey game as well?"

"So far the deaths correspond with the hockey games. She was probably drunk and wasn't worried about going with him. If she wasn't dead, she'd be saying he didn't seem scary or strange," Celeste said.

"None of them seem strange until you're tied up and being hacked to death."

Celeste headed towards the rink. She nodded. "If all the killers, rapists and molesters of the world looked like they truly were inside, no one would ever be fooled."

Adam sank into silence.

* * * *

They stood outside the arena and Celeste looked around, trying to find a trace of the killer. Her attention was divided between Adam and Tomas. Adam kept her nipples at attention. Her skin felt hot and itchy. She wanted him. She couldn't go an hour without remembering his mouth on hers, his body pressed against hers and his cock ramming into her pussy.

Adam was the first mortal she'd been this attracted to in years, and she had the uneasy instinct that her emotions were more than just lust. Yet it was more than a need for his body. Adam challenged her mind as much as he pleasured her, and it had been very rare for a mortal to do so. From the moment they'd met, she'd known Adam could come to mean something more than just a good fuck.

He questioned her about everything, and no one else did that. They always accepted what she had to say. Maybe it was because she tended to intimidate the people around her, and they were too scared to ask her about her actions and motives. Adam was neither of those things, and he stood up to her when he wanted answers. It was those differences that worried her because she could easily fall in love with him.

Since there was no one around, Celeste grabbed Adam's arm, then pulled him into a hidden corner. Wrapping her arms around his neck, she kissed him fiercely.

"Celeste, wait." Adam pulled away slightly. "Someone might see us."

"You don't want anyone to see your bare ass?" Celeste needed more power to be able to find any hints of whether or not Tomas had been around, and having sex with Adam would give her the boost she needed. Plus, she couldn't seem to keep her hands off him.

She'd used enough of her power earlier that night while talking to Tomas at the crime scene, she didn't have enough to catch any lingering traces of the fallen.

"Darling, we can do this without my getting naked."
Adam laughed.

He ground his hips into hers. She moaned as he
unbuttoned her shirt. Adam pushed her bra up as he
continued to thrust his jean-covered cock against her.
He took her breasts captive, squeezing and massaging
them. Adam plucked her nipples.

He bit her neck gently. Working his way down to
her tits, he covered her right nipple with his mouth.
He slid his hands down her smooth stomach to the
snap on her jeans. Celeste arched her back as Adam
began to nip at her.

Forcing him to lean back against the wall, Celeste
smiled at him. She trailed her lips down his neck.
Pushing up his shirt, she rubbed her hands over his
well-muscled chest. His small nipples stiffened as she
flicked them with her fingernails. He groaned softly.
Delighted with his response, Celeste laughed.
Kneeling, she met his eyes as she unsnapped his jeans.

Adam's green eyes were glowing with passion and
something else—Celeste wasn't sure she wanted to
find out what that something else was. How foolish
she was to have got involved with him. She broke
contact and turned her eyes to the cock in front of her.

She sucked him into her mouth. She nibbled from
the tip to the base, including little tastes of his balls.
With each suck, his hips began to move more quickly.
Threading his fingers in her silky hair, he started to
thrust in earnest.

Celeste tilted her gaze up to see his face. His head
was braced against the concrete wall and his lips were
pulled back in a grimace. If she didn't know better,
she would have thought he was in pain. But by the
speed of his hips, she knew it was only a matter of
time before he came.

She built the pressure until Adam couldn't contain a deep groan. He thrust deeply, and his hot cum spurted into her mouth. She swallowed until he was done. One last jerk of his hips then he pulled his cock from her mouth. Sinking down to his knees, he faced her.

"Why did we come here, Celeste?" Adam asked her. "There are more comfortable places for us to fuck."

"Sorry. I just couldn't wait any longer." Celeste shook her head. "I can't believe I did that here while we're looking for Tomas."

Though she'd let her lust take over, there had been another reason why she'd chosen to give Adam a blow job in the alley. It wasn't something she did very often.

Adam cupped her face, then met her gaze. "No harm done, I guess, but we should probably get on with whatever you wanted to do here."

Celeste reached out with her senses, and found a trace of Tomas here. He had grabbed the women right outside Joe Louis. The women hadn't protested or argued and no one remembered seeing a couple fighting. Tomas must have used a little magic to convince them to go with him.

When the fallen went over to madness, their eyes became black holes sucking all light and colour into them. Tomas couldn't hide who and what he was from mortals unless he used some of his power to disguise his intention. Like all fallen, he was incredibly handsome and could act normally to achieve his goal, but using power left traces for Celeste to follow. She could only hope she was able to find Tomas before he killed again.

"What are you doing?"

"Tomas was here." After standing, Celeste fixed her shirt then buttoned her jeans. She gestured for Adam to stand. Moving to the sidewalk, she looked south.

"We know that. He picks them up at games."

"No, he picked the last one up at this entrance." She circled slowly, like a bloodhound looking for a scent.

"How do you know?" Adam sounded sceptical.

"I can feel him. Your climax helped me grab a trace of him. He took her then headed south."

"What the hell are you talking about?"

Celeste glanced at him for a moment. Shrugging, she faced south again. "I can't build my power in the normal way."

"The normal way?"

"I can't pray to Him for help. Why would He want to help me? So I get my power in other ways."

Adam frowned. "What other ways?"

"Usually from sex. I harness it until I need it."

"Right." Adam didn't sound convinced.

"Well, there are less pleasurable ways to gather power, but I choose to do it without harming the other person. Angels aren't supposed to cause harm, even fallen. Yet some of my former brethren have lost their sanity because of their separation from God. Those fallen will hurt or kill any mortal they can."

"If I accept that you're a fallen angel, then I have to accept the fact that you will never need me."

Celeste frowned at him. "Never need you? I need you to help me find Tomas."

"No, you don't. I'm sure you can trace him no matter what happens to me. You can use any man as long as he's willing to have sex with you." Bitterness filled his voice.

"You're right, I don't need you, but since I can't seem to keep my hands off you, I might as well enjoy myself. It was the orgasm you gave me in the limo that allowed me to connect with Tomas for the first time the other night. Unfortunately, I wasn't able to see where he was." Celeste rested her hand on his shoulder. "But I'm glad you're the one here. You help me in more ways than just sex."

"That's why you brought me here. We'll have a little fun, I'll get a blow job, you'll get some power and we'll find Tomas." Adam stalked out of the alley, then turned back when she didn't follow him. "Aren't you coming? Haven't you figured out where he is? That way you won't have to touch or deal with me anymore."

"What the hell is your problem? I thought you were the one who always wanted no strings attached. You never wanted to get involved in a real relationship with anyone." Celeste was puzzled. What had happened in Adam's mind to make him start acting like a spoilt brat? He was getting mind-blowing sex with someone he thought wasn't going to stick around afterwards. Wasn't that every man's dream?

She couldn't believe he was so angry. She was offering what he had always said he wanted — sex without attachments. Was he upset because he thought he wasn't going to be the one walking away? She knew there was power in being the one to make the decision to end it. He would have no control over the way the relationship would go.

Celeste caught up to him but didn't say anything as she slid into her car. He stood outside and stared down at her.

"Are you coming with me?"

"Where are you going?"

Celeste shrugged. "I'm driving around for a little bit. I have a slight trace on him, but I need to be closer to get a better direction."

"You mean the blow job didn't do the trick?" he said nastily.

Celeste quirked an eyebrow at him. "Are we going to be bitchy about this whole thing? I can't tell you I'm sorry. You would know I was lying to you. I need the power sex can give me. I am sorry if you don't understand how it works. I can't explain it to you."

"Can't or won't?"

"Both. You're human. You have no right and no need to hear about the power the fallen have." Celeste started the car.

"Why not?"

"The workings of angels, even fallen angels, are far above the minds of men. I told you about me because I can't seem to lie to you, but trust me, there are places you don't want to go, Adam." Celeste's voice was soft as memories of the beauty of the places she'd seen danced through her mind.

Adam laughed harshly. "What can you do to me that any human couldn't?"

Celeste's eyes filled with tears and a bitter knowledge. "I've seen the loss of Heaven, Adam. I've seen what it can do to angels and humans alike. I've heard the screams of those who have lost their souls. I've watched them slowly understand and accept their banishment, not from Heaven, which is bad enough, but from the very presence of Him." Tears spilled down Celeste's face. "I can take you to the place, Adam. I can show you Hell. There is no rest for the wicked or the weary, Adam. I've figured that out on my own."

Adam felt his anger weaken. There was an emptiness shining in Celeste's eyes. A sorrow hung heavy in her heart. How could an angel live outside the presence of God without going mad? He was afraid to look too closely at her soul. He found he held a hope in his heart that she would somehow see her way to staying with him. Could an angel who would always wish for Heaven and the presence of God be happy with a mortal?

His heart ached. Celeste Young had lived for centuries longing for the one thing she would never have again. Did he have what it took to fill that emptiness in her heart? Did he want to try filling it?

He shook his head. "I'll catch a cab back to my house, Celeste. I can't deal with this right now and I need to check the rest of my businesses. If I'm not visible, there are others who will try to take over, and they aren't men I would want running my city."

"And you are?" Celeste asked.

"Yes, I am. There are things I won't do, just as there are a lot of things that I am willing to allow. As long as the city doesn't burn and the dead don't start walking, I'm doing my job. There is a balance that must be kept."

"Jakar did say he was here to help you do that. True demons fear unbalance."

"True demons? What rabbit hole have I fallen down? I can't believe this. Not only have I slept with a fallen angel, my right hand man is a fucking demon." Adam shook his head in disbelief. Angels and demons weren't part of his normal daily routine, and it gave his mind a lot to process — he wasn't even able to work up the energy to be surprised by the knowledge that Jakar was a demon.

"Just keep an eye on Jakar. So far, you are doing what he wants. If you upset him, he could kill you."

"Jakar wouldn't touch me. Not if I threaten him with you." Adam grinned.

"I'm just as dangerous as your pet demon, Adam. I could kill you with a simple thought. Do you have enough confidence in yourself to be able to deal with that? Will you trust me enough to believe I would never hurt you willingly?"

Adam watched Celeste drive away from him then flagged down a cab. Instead of heading home, he went to the only place he knew of to find some answers.

Chapter Seven

It had been a long time since Adam had set foot in a church. Standing in the vestibule, he stared up at the large stained glass window behind the altar. The light from the setting sun caused the colours to flare in streaming reds and yellows down the aisles. There was a feeling of timelessness about Saint Anne de Detroit Church. Adam could almost feel the prayers of the people who came every Sunday to talk to God. He turned as a door opened to his left.

An elderly man dressed in black with a white collar greeted him. "How are you today, sir?"

Adam shook the man's hand. "I'm fine, Father."

"You are not one of my regular worshippers. I would remember a face like yours. Why do you come here?"

"I have some questions, Father. This church is on my way home and I thought I could ask you for the answers."

"Ask me if you must. I can't promise to have the answers for you. There are some things that defy explanation. I am Father Michael." The priest gestured for Adam to follow him into his small office. "Can I offer you coffee, my young friend?"

Adam wanted something stronger, but didn't think the priest would have any whisky. "Coffee will be fine, Father."

"I would offer you a stronger drink, but we are here in the church and He tends to frown upon His priests getting sloshed." Michael's wrinkled face broke into a grin while his brilliant grey eyes sparkled at Adam.

Had the priest read his mind? He took the mug when it was offered to him. Michael had fixed it the way Adam liked it. Narrowing his eyes, he wondered if he had ever seen the man before.

"I don't know you from Adam," the old man said, chuckling.

"How did you know my name?" Getting nervous, Adam started to stand.

The priest waved him back to his seat. "Even an old priest who rarely leaves his church knows the name of the leader of the Demons. It pays to know your enemies."

Adam was puzzled. "Enemies? I haven't done anything to this church or you before. How can I be your enemy?"

"You condone violence against your fellow man. You live the old adage, an eye for an eye. Every night, my parishioners hear those words while they are out on the streets and they seek to take vengeance on those who have harmed them. How can you not be my enemy?"

"Then why allow me to come in here? Why talk to me and treat me as a guest?" Adam demanded.

"Even Jesus sat down with Judas, Adam." Father Michael studied him. He seemed to know how his words were affecting Adam. "Sit and talk to me a while. Tell me what it is you wish to know."

Adam took a deep drink of coffee. He peered at the cross on the wall behind the priest. He wouldn't feel guilty for what he had done to survive. The world was a hard place and he'd had to be strong to make it as far as he had.

"I've met someone."

The priest looked a little surprised. "Have you come here asking for relationship advice?" He chuckled. "I must admit I would have thought that a man like you would have no problems with women."

"You would have to meet Celeste to understand why I need some answers."

"Miss Celeste Young?" The gleam in the priest's eyes suggested that he knew Celeste quite well.

"Yes. Do you know her?"

Michael nodded slightly. "Let's just say I know of her. What has she done to confuse you?"

"It's what she says she is that's confusing."

The priest didn't say a word, just lifted an eyebrow in question.

"She tells me that she's a fallen angel." Adam ducked his head. He couldn't believe he was actually contemplating accepting her story.

"There are more things under heaven and earth than we will ever know," Father Michael said. "Excuse me for paraphrasing Shakespeare, but the bard was right. Why do you think she's lying?"

"I don't believe in angels, fallen or otherwise."

"And yet you are willing to accept demons?"

"I can deal with demons. I've dealt with human ones all my life. I've never had anything to do with angels." After standing, Adam moved around the office.

"True. Your line of work doesn't lend itself to dealing with good people." Michael stared into the fire burning cheerfully in the fireplace. "What do you want to know?"

"Is she crazy?"

"Celeste?" Michael laughed. "No, my son, she isn't crazy. At least not yet. She has managed to keep her mind through all these years."

"Then you think she is an angel?"

"Yes, Adam. I know she's an angel. But not a card carrying, flaming sword and golden winged angel. All that was taken from her the moment she left Heaven." There was a melancholy tone in the priest's voice. "Now in many ways, she is no different than you or I."

Adam didn't say anything. He studied the old man, trying to decide if he could believe him.

"I can tell you the legend of the Fall of Lucifer if you wish. Maybe it would help you to decide."

"Tell me, Father. Of course, then I'll have to decide if I truly believe in Heaven." Adam reclaimed his seat by the fire.

Father Michael stared into the flames for a moment, as if gathering his thoughts. Sighing, he said, "I can't convince you of the reality of Heaven, Adam. You will have to see it for yourself. But know this—Celeste Young will never see Heaven again. She forfeited her right when she listened to the lies of the Daystar."

"Daystar?"

Father Michael nodded. "Lucifer, or the Daystar, was the most beloved of the angels. He was even more beloved than God's own archangels."

"Bet that caused some jealousy," Adam muttered, thinking of how his men fought amongst each other to gain his favour.

"Why would it? They were created to adore God. The archangels were made to perform His requests and enforce His laws. They weren't made to be jealous or angry over any favour that He might bestow on another."

"Seems something went wrong if Lucifer decided he wasn't happy with things."

"It went horribly wrong. Lucifer became jealous of the power that God gave to Jesus. He also hated the love the Father had for the fragile mortals He had created. Lucifer was truly the first creature who ever thought about himself. He thought what he wanted was the most important thing. He cared nothing for others, only what he could get. He wanted the power that God had, so he decided to take it from Him. He raised an army and tried to overthrow God. The battle between the Host of Heaven and Lucifer's army was fierce, but in the end the Host won. Lucifer and his followers were cast out of Heaven, never to return. The fallen ease their torment by hurting the mortals God loves so much."

"What about Celeste? She says she's a fallen who has repented, but for some reason, God won't let her back. She says that she's an Enforcer, one of those who hunt down the fallen that have turned and killed mortals. Who are the Enforcers and why won't God let them back into Heaven?"

Father Michael looked at Adam with sorrow in his grey eyes. A sorrow that told Adam the priest had a deep understanding of how the loss had affected Celeste. "The Enforcers are merely legends as far as the church is concerned. We have no real proof that they exist."

"But if the Enforcers don't exist, how do you know that the fallen do?"

The priest laughed. "You're right. We don't have proof that the fallen exist at all. Maybe they are all legends made up to make easy the explanations for evil and cruelty that exist in the world."

"The Enforcers?"

"The legends state that there were some of the rebellious angels who repented after the fall. They begged God to allow them back."

"And God said no. Why would He do that? If God is supposed to be forgiving and loving, why would He turn His back on those who begged forgiveness?"

Again, there was a flash of sorrow and puzzlement in the priest's eyes. He shrugged then said, "I don't know. Only God knows what our purpose here in the world is. He must have a reason to deny them. So, they set out to right the wrongs they've created by hunting down the fallen who have gone over the edge. They hunt to get rid of the killers and rapists. Only the Enforcers have enough power to end the fallen angels' reign."

"Okay. Where are her wings?"

Father Michael laughed. "If you check her shoulder blades closely, Adam, I'm sure you will find two small scars. Those scars are all that's left of her wings."

"Do you believe all of this? I suppose you must because you're a priest." Adam still wasn't sure whether he believed any of it.

"It doesn't matter what I believe, Adam. It only matters what you choose to do with the knowledge. You could walk away from her and have nothing to do with her ever again, which would be easier on both of you. Or you can choose to stay, believing she's crazy, and enjoy what time you have together." Father Michael stood, indicating that the meeting was over.

"Now, if you will excuse me, it's way past this old man's bed time. I'll walk with you to the door."

Adam thanked the priest and followed him out into the vestibule. He turned to hand Father Michael a donation. A beam of moonlight drifted through the stained glass window behind the altar. It landed on the priest's face. Suddenly, the old, slightly stooped man was transformed into a tall, eternally young man with brilliant silver eyes and a stern countenance. Adam felt awe-struck as he looked at him.

"One last word, my son. Don't allow your doubts and fears to hide the urgency. Tomas must be stopped. With each woman he kills, his power grows. Celeste knows this and she will do what she must to end it. Be her strength."

Adam nodded. He swung around to leave the church. Then he remembered the money in his hand. Turning back, he gasped. The priest had disappeared. There hadn't been enough time for him to get out of sight.

Adam stumbled from the church and waved down a cab. What a strange experience, and he wasn't sure what to make of it all. Who had the priest been? Where had he gone? He wasn't entirely sure he wanted to know.

* * * *

Jakar met him at the door, and studied him.

"Have you learnt anything?" Jakar asked as he followed Adam into the study.

Adam flung himself down onto the leather sofa in front of the fireplace. "She's a fallen angel, and uses sex to build whatever kind of power she has. I'm pretty sure we probably shouldn't be together at all, but there's something about Celeste that I can't get enough of."

"Trust me. Don't make the mistake of falling in love with her. Loving a fallen isn't easy, and Celeste knows that. She has seen other fallen try to live a 'normal' life. A life she wishes with all her heart she could have, but knows she can't. There is madness haunting her soul and she feels its grip grow tighter every day." Jakar poured Adam a glass of whisky, then handed it to him.

"What does a demon know about the torment of a fallen angel?" At Jakar's start of surprise, Adam grinned. Staring down into the amber liquid, he searched for answers he knew he would never find at the bottom of the glass. "She warned me not to trust you. You warn me not to trust her. It's a good thing I don't trust anyone."

"I'm a true demon. I have been around since the beginning of time, Montgomery. When the angels were banished from Heaven, many of them turned into demons. They took Lucifer as their king and decided that tormenting humans would make their miserable lives better. They made it hard for us.

"Angels have always existed. So have demons. There is a balance in everything. We've always managed to keep it that way. But with the fallen, the balance isn't there. There is truly nothing to keep them in check except for those marked with the brand of Cain."

Adam remembered the cross on Celeste's breast. "She told me about that. So she has decided to help save humans from the fallen. Why would she choose to do that? Why would she put herself at risk for people who don't even know she exists? Why kill her own kind?"

"In a way, it is redemption for what she has done. Not all of them choose to try and make up for their mistakes. I think that only the strongest try. The rest have taken the easiest way out by being evil. I know I can't make you believe if you choose not to. The fallen have managed to stay hidden for thousands of years, so mortals don't believe in them anymore. The saying that the greatest trick the Devil ever played was to make people believe he didn't exist is true. The fallen have convinced mortals that they aren't real, so when a mere mortal is confronted by the knowledge, it takes an Act of God to make them believe." He poured Adam another drink then left.

As the flames danced in front of him, Adam tried to organise his scattered thoughts.

Chapter Eight

Adam stared out into the darkness of the city below him. For hours, he had prowled his house, trying to find some peace from the questions plaguing him. There were no answers to be found. Damn, women could screw up a man's life. He had loved his mother and she had left him, betraying his tender heart by dying at his father's hands. Then he'd spent the next five years moving from foster home to foster home until he'd run away. Who knew he'd find a better life on the street than he had in the foster system? Now there was all of this with Celeste. The shadows closed in around him and he leaned his forehead against the cool glass.

"What do you see when you look out there?" Celeste's voice came from the darkness of his bed.

Adam whirled around to find her curled up in the middle of the mattress, her blue eyes fixed on his naked body. "How the hell did you get in here? I know for a fact that Jakar would never have let you in."

"Who said I needed him to let me in? He would never try to stop me." Celeste shrugged. "Your friend fears me, Adam."

"He should, shouldn't he? If he got in your way, you would destroy him without a thought. He's nothing to you."

"That's true. Jakar doesn't mean anything to me. But he means something to you. That is why I wouldn't hurt him. By destroying him, I would destroy a piece of you and I would never intentionally hurt you."

Adam turned away to study the shadows again. "You can't hurt me unless I let you. What makes you think you have that much power over me?"

"Maybe I don't. Maybe all we have is great sex, Adam. If that's the truth, then why can't we enjoy what we have and not look to the end?" The rustle of the sheets told him she was moving.

Adam held his hand up to stop her. Shaking his head, he growled angrily. "Do I look like an idiot, Celeste? If you truly are what you say you are, you can make me do whatever you want. A being with the power you have can control anyone."

"That's true. I could make you climb into bed with me. I could make you fuck me until we both can barely move. But when free will is taken, there is no joy in the choice."

"You want me to choose to fuck you. You want me to choose to betray myself." Adam laughed harshly as he studied her reflection in the window. "What choice is there in that?"

"None, I guess. What do you see when you look in the shadows, Adam?" Her voice was compelling. She seemed to want to know what haunted his soul.

"I see my father." Adam watched the scene unravel before him. "I was only seven when my father killed my mother. I stood in the corner of the kitchen and watched while he beat her. One particularly vicious blow caused Mom to fall and on the way down, she hit her head on the edge of the table. We both just stood there for a few minutes, waiting for her to stand up again. When Dad looked at me, I ran and hid in my room with the door locked. Dad could have gotten in if he wanted to, but I never saw him again.

"Three days later, the police broke into the house and took me away. There was blood in the kitchen, but Mom was missing. I waited for months, thinking there had been a mistake. I didn't believe Mom would abandon me to strangers. Then one night, I realised she wasn't ever coming back because Dad had killed her that night, and got rid of the body."

Adam inhaled sharply. "I learnt the truth about love. Mom had loved Dad so much she would never have thought about leaving him. Mom never left Dad, and she allowed us to stay in that abusive home because of her inability to love me more than my father. She betrayed me for my father and that's when I learnt love only leads to betrayal."

He stiffened as she wrapped her arms around his waist. He felt her wet cheeks rest against his back.

"Don't waste your tears on me, Celeste. There are thousands of people out in the world who have had worse lives than me. I've managed to overcome my beginnings. That's all that's important."

"But you can't forget your past. You live with those memories every day."

"Those memories are what made me what I am. I would never get rid of them because they tell me I can only trust myself. Everyone is out to get something." He stopped Celeste's protest. "Yes, Celeste. Everyone wants something from me."

Celeste couldn't deny that. She had used him for the power she needed to stop Tomas, but that didn't mean she didn't care for him. In fact, Celeste knew she was in danger of falling in love with him. *Oh hell*, she thought to herself, *I might as well admit I already do love him. My heart is going to bleed after this one leaves me.*

She pressed her lips to his warm back. She turned him to face her. Reaching up, she held his face in her hands and gently whispered a kiss across his lips. She felt his heart pound with a heavy beat. She wrapped his body in her arms and tried to comfort him.

Adam pushed her away. He stalked to the bed and sat down. "Why won't you leave? I really don't want you here."

"Ah, sometimes we don't get what we want."

Even though he'd said he wanted her to leave, she knew he really didn't mean it, and she wasn't going let him wallow in his anger and sorrow anymore. She'd learnt the hard way that letting the past define her present was the easiest way to lose her mind. She wasn't going to let Adam do it tonight.

The rest of Celeste's clothes faded away. She parted Adam's legs and knelt between them. She was going to make this loving slow and gentle to ease the pain hiding inside Adam's heart. She knew part of it was her nature. As a former angel, she didn't like to see anyone suffer. But Celeste knew that wasn't the entire reason why she needed to feel Adam inside her that night. She knew she loved him. He had managed to break the protective layer around her heart by always being honest with her. While he might not completely believe everything she told him, Adam hadn't walked away. He stayed with her to help, and because of that, she would do anything to make him happy.

She slid her hands up his thighs. Cupping his balls gently, she squeezed them as she stroked his cock with her other hand. Celeste wanted to give him something good to think about, and this time it wasn't about getting anything for herself. It was about making Adam feel good.

He leant back on his elbows. A quiet part of Adam's mind told him not to allow her to do this to him, yet the majority of his brain said to let her. That making love to Celeste would help take the anger away. He still wasn't entirely sure what he was going to do about their relationship, but most of the time, he felt better after being with her. He knew Celeste was slowly taking over his soul. The more time they spent together, the more it was going to hurt when she left him. He groaned softly as she circled his cock with her full lips, then slid down his length.

"Don't think, Adam. Forget everything else for a while. Focus on me and what I'm doing." Her voice was soft and smooth.

"What you're doing is driving me crazy," he moaned.

She laughed. He could feel her smile wrap around his cock. Her warm mouth massaged his aching dick. He tried to keep a distance between them—tried to remember she was doing this out of pity. Celeste didn't really love him. Then the slow, hard suction of her mouth seemed to suck all the thoughts from his head. It didn't matter whether she was doing this because she loved him or pitied him. He was just going to enjoy it.

He tangled his hands in her hair and thrust his hips up. He wanted to take control and fuck her mouth hard and fast. Celeste was surprisingly strong. She pushed his hips back to the bed and slowed her movements.

His protest got stuck in his throat as she slid from his cock and licked his balls. She made her way up his body, teasing him with gentle bites, wet kisses and licks.

It seemed like every move Celeste made was deliberate. She helped Adam lay back on the bed then made her way down from his forehead to his feet, taking nips and sucks along the way. She took control of the lovemaking. He started to reach for her but she pushed his hands to the bed and shook her head.

"No touching. Let me do the work this time, Adam," she whispered seductively in the dark.

He didn't argue as she straddled his hips. Taking him into her hand, she lowered herself onto him. He couldn't keep from moaning as her moist heat enveloped his cock. Adam had never had a lover be so gentle. The silken slide of his cock in and out of her pussy started a pressure building in his head. He longed to grab her hips and start plunging into her, but he savoured giving up control to the beautiful woman riding him.

Celeste arched her back, pushing her breasts out. Cupping them with her hands, she stroked and tweaked her nipples. She leant forward to grip his shoulder and pushed her nipple into his mouth. He latched on and sucked hard, wringing a soft cry from her. Adam used his teeth and his tongue to drive her higher.

He couldn't seem to get deep enough inside her. Finally, his self-control broke and he grabbed her hips. He knew he'd leave bruises where he gripped her, he slammed her down on him. The time for gentleness was over, he needed to come and he wanted her to be right there with him when he did.

He yelled as the pressure exploded throughout his body. He faintly heard Celeste scream as she came. His muscles relaxed and as he slid willingly into sleep, he heard Celeste whisper, "Rest," then he felt her kiss his forehead.

* * * *

Celeste opened her apartment door and sighed. It had been a long twenty-four hours. She should have been relaxed after the lovemaking session with Adam, but she just felt discouraged and sad. By the Power, her heart was a fickle thing. No matter how many times she had told herself she wouldn't fall in love, here she was again. Caught up in the middle of a heartbreak without any way of saving herself.

"Look what the cat dragged in," a warm voice spoke up from the living room.

Celeste looked up to see William standing in the middle of the room, his arms crossed over his chest while she moved slowly towards him. He embraced her and she rested her forehead against his thick chest. He made soothing sounds in his throat as he stroked her hair.

He pulled back from Celeste and her eyes filled with tears as all the emotions she'd been trying to hold back flooded her. "Come now, Celeste. What's this? I haven't seen you cry since we realised we weren't going back to Heaven. What's happened?"

"Nothing. I'm tired. I need to go take a shower." Not wanting to discuss Adam and their relationship at the moment, Celeste wiped the tears from her cheeks, then started to walk towards her bedroom. With a puzzled frown, she turned back to him. "What are you doing here?"

"I had a visit from our friendly pain in the ass. He said you might need my help with a problem." William walked to her, then tipped her chin up with his finger. He whispered a gentle kiss on her cheek. "I see that Mika'il was right. You do need my help. You are more than just tired, my angel. You are heartsick. Want to tell me what's wrong?"

Celeste shook her head. "No. It doesn't matter in the grand scheme of things. I'll get over it. Let me take a shower and sleep for a little while. Then we can start looking for Tomas."

"So it is Tomas. I was wondering when the slippery son-of-a-bitch was going to show his face again." Grimacing, William pushed Celeste down the hall. "Go and clean up. When you get out of the shower, you can bring me up to date, then take a nap."

"What will you do while I'm napping?" Celeste asked suspiciously.

"I'll be doing what I do best. I'll start gathering information."

Celeste didn't argue. She went into the bathroom and shut the door. There had been few moments in her life when she could let down her guard, but with William here, she could relax. He could take care of himself. Climbing under the hot water, she allowed the heat to surround her.

William waited until he heard the shower start then he headed to the kitchen. He had visited Celeste several times over the years she had lived in Detroit, and he was as familiar with her apartment as he was with his own. He was humming softly to himself when the phone rang.

"Hello."

A tense silence came over the line. "Who is this?"

"Depends on who you were calling and who's asking the question." William continued to make breakfast.

"I need to talk to Celeste now." The commanding tone of the man's voice told William the stranger was used to having his demands met.

William could feel the anger start to build in the man on the other end of the line. "She's busy at the moment. Can I take a message?"

"Who the hell are you?" There was an unsure tone in the man's voice.

"I'm William. I'm a good friend of Celeste's." He could almost hear the caller grinding his teeth.

"Tell her Adam called." Adam slammed down the phone.

Shrugging, William hung up. Boy, was that guy tense. He continued to make breakfast while waiting for Celeste to get out of the shower. Twenty minutes later, the door opened and Celeste came out. Her black nightie barely reached her thighs. He gestured to the table where a plate full of eggs, toast and bacon sat. Smiling, she picked up a piece of bacon.

"If I was so inclined, Celeste, you would find me hard pressed to keep my hands off you." William grinned at her.

Celeste didn't even glance at him. She shovelled the food in.

"How long since you've eaten, angel?" William leaned against the counter and watched her.

"I don't remember," she muttered.

"Hey, some guy named Adam called while you were in the shower and by the way he sounded, I think he'll be showing up just about now."

A pounding sounded on the door. William motioned for Celeste to stay seated. He sauntered to the door, opening it just as Adam was raising his fist to pound again.

Reaching out, William grabbed Adam's arm to jerk him in the room. "Don't you have any respect for the other people in this building? They could probably feel you knocking through their doors."

Chapter Nine

Adam yanked his arm out of William's grip and looked around. He saw the dark-haired man point to the kitchen. Stalking over, he found his anger growing. It exploded when he found Celeste calmly eating breakfast wearing a see-through nightie and a just-got-out-of-the-shower look.

"Damn, Celeste. You fuck me unconscious, then run home to fuck some other guy." He could feel his hands trembling.

Celeste didn't react to him. She kept on eating while the stranger chuckled.

"I'm not just 'some guy'. I happen to be very important to her."

Celeste glared at the other man. "You aren't making this better by acting like that."

William quirked an eyebrow at her. "Angel, he certainly acts like he owns you."

Adam whirled around to face William. "Who the hell are you really?"

"My name is William Bradford. I am one of Celeste's oldest friends." William bowed slightly.

Adam ran a hand through his hair. "Hell, you're one of them, aren't you?"

"One of them?"

"A fallen angel."

William shrugged. "I really no longer think of myself as anything."

"You're not a fallen angel?"

"Yes, I am, but I am also an Enforcer." William rubbed his hand over his chest. "To be honest, though, I try not to involve myself in any of the petty squabbles going on between our brethren."

"Then why are you here?" He moved to stand beside Celeste. He placed a hand on her shoulder, a silent signal to William that he'd claimed her.

Celeste didn't move to shrug off the hand, and Adam could see the exhaustion in her face. He started to crouch beside her, but William pushed him out of the way in time to catch Celeste as she toppled over.

Lifting her in his arms, he told Adam, "Stay there. I'll be back to explain some things to you." William headed off down the hall to Celeste's room.

Adam wanted to follow, but understood that he didn't have the right to do that. He didn't really have any rights at all when it came to Celeste, no matter how many times they'd slept together. But he wanted to be the one to take care of her when she needed help. He prowled around Celeste's living room while he waited.

"All right, Adam." William joined him. "Do you want to hit me now or talk like civilised people about this whole thing?"

"There's nothing to talk about. Celeste doesn't owe me any explanation. What she does when she isn't with me is none of my business."

"Now you say something like that. Why didn't you say it while she was awake and could hear you?" William waved Adam to the couch. "Sit down. Get me up to speed about Tomas. We need to catch him soon or we'll be in big trouble."

"If you don't consider yourself a fallen or an Enforcer, why the hell are you even here?" Adam demanded.

William sighed. "A mutual friend suggested that Celeste might need some help. Since she is my only friend in this God-forsaken world, I decided to heed his warning and come for a visit. Just in time, too."

"What's that supposed to mean?"

"She's running herself to exhaustion. She's dealing with you and trying to get a lead on Tomas at the same time. She is constantly sending out bits of power, searching for Tomas. When she first arrived here, and realised what Tomas was doing, she used her power to set a net over the city, and each surge of emotion Tomas feels affects it. She's replenishing the spell every second from her own power. I think he's found a way to tap into the spell and has been stealing power from her. Which could be why she's having such a hard time finding him."

William stared at Adam. "If it were me, I would leave Tomas alone. I have never understood this attachment she has to mortals."

"You don't have any human friends?"

"I only use mortals for one thing and it isn't friendship. So tell me, what do you know about Tomas so far?"

"He picks the women up at the hockey games."

"Hmmm…there's a game tonight. I wonder if he'll kill again. What's his pattern? How long does he go between killing?"

"Every three or four days, from what we can find out. It doesn't help that the Wings have been playing at home a lot."

William didn't answer. He stared off into space. "Even if you two fucked like bunnies all day, Celeste isn't going to be up to full strength by tonight. I guess I'll be the one out gathering clues."

"Full strength?" Adam was puzzled. They'd had mind-blowing sex last night. Why hadn't she gathered power then?

"Why do you think she collapsed a few minutes ago? She ran out."

"But last night..."

"Her mind must have been on something other than gathering power. And that's why she needs me here. You're distracting her. Why don't you go home for a while? She'll be up in a couple hours. Then come and get her, take her out for a relaxing afternoon. Try and keep her mind off of Tomas. I'll be out looking around."

Adam started to head for the door. Stopping, he turned around to ask something, but stopped himself. Then he turned back towards the door.

"Go ahead and ask. But are you sure you'll believe my answer?"

Facing the door, Adam took a deep breath. He wasn't sure he could bring himself to ask.

"No, we haven't. And we never will." William's voice was filled with understanding. "Celeste is my dearest friend and the only one I'll ever trust. I won't destroy that connection by turning it into a physical one."

Adam nodded in thanks then left.

* * * *

Two hours later, Celeste had just finished lunch when another knock sounded on her door. Her body was rested, but her power was still very low. This time there wasn't any anger in the sound. She opened it to find Adam leaning casually on the doorjamb. *He looks good enough to eat.* In tight, faded blue jeans and a white T-shirt, he looked more relaxed. She had to fight the urge to pull him inside and run her hands all over his naked body. She grinned at him.

She could see the lust burning in his eyes. He shook his head and disappointment ran through her.

"Grab a jacket. I'm kidnapping you."

"Really? And where are you taking me?"

"You'll just have to wait and see." He smirked at her. As he helped her with her jacket, he caressed her shoulders.

"It's a surprise, huh?" She shut the door behind her. Following him to his truck, she mentally wiped the drool off her chin. The man had an ass she would love to lick chocolate off. She backed off from those thoughts. She had the feeling Adam was trying to help her relax, and having lustful thoughts wasn't going to help lower her heart rate.

His hand brushed her breast as he helped her into the truck. It took all her will power not to grab his hand and cup it around her breast. She was disgusted with herself—she couldn't even go five minutes without thinking some kind of sexual thought about this man. She was going to have to do better.

The silence in the truck was thick as they headed down the street. Finally, Celeste laughed. "We don't seem to be able to talk to each other unless we're arguing or fucking, huh? Or if we're discussing this case?"

He chuckled. "I'm sure we could if we tried. We've just never had the chance, I guess."

"Did you ever finish high school?" Celeste asked, turning in her seat to look at him.

He shook his head. "You're looking at a self-made man. Of course, in a street gang, you really don't need a degree to get where you want to go."

"But you do need to be intelligent and cunning," Celeste stated.

"Just like any animal living in the jungle."

"I give you credit. You didn't start out with much, but somehow you managed to gain a lot."

"By stealing, cheating and lying. Yeah, that makes me a model citizen. Isn't that against your angelic code?"

Celeste gave him a slight smile. "Maybe if I was still an angel I'd have a problem with it. But I've lived in the world for a long time. You have a strong survival instinct. You do whatever you have to do to make it day by day."

"Don't throw stones in a glass house."

"I'm not going to judge you, that's for sure. Considering what I'm being punished for, your crimes are pretty petty."

Adam laughed. "I don't think the police would agree with you."

"True. Some of them have no room to criticise you either. The only one you will ever have to answer to in the end is Him."

"Why don't you call him God?"

"Getting tossed from Heaven puts a dampener on things. Since I can no longer stand in His presence, I can't even say His name. It hurts my head and my heart."

"I wouldn't know what it's like to be banished like that. I mean, I'm sure it's like being banished from a parent's presence. But since neither of my parents cared for me, I've always known that feeling." Adam shrugged. He pulled into the parking garage.

Celeste looked around. "The zoo? You're taking me to the zoo. I've never been here before."

"You've been in Detroit for ten years and have never been to the zoo. Amazing." Adam took her hand and dragged her to the entrance.

"I donated money for the new polar bear exhibit, doesn't that count for something?" She laughed.

"No, you have to actually see the bears. It's a great exhibit, but first we have to go and see the penguins."

"Why?"

"Whenever I come here, I stop by the penguin house first. I love penguins."

Celeste blinked, trying to reconcile the image of the tough gang boss with the image of a man who loved penguins. Shaking her head, she laughed. It didn't matter. *Just enjoy the day*, she told herself as they walked towards the exhibits.

* * * *

Celeste dropped on her couch. She was exhausted. Adam had run her all over the zoo, checking out the animals. They had laughed, kissed and spent the entire afternoon being normal and it was late when they got back to her apartment. Adam was in the kitchen putting the take-out Chinese on plates. It was just the kind of afternoon she'd needed to restore her energy. Now was the time to build her power.

Adam put the plate on the coffee table in front of her. He smiled at the contented look on her face.

The food was forgotten as Celeste led Adam into her bedroom. She smiled up at him. Somehow, they had managed to keep their hands off each other at the zoo, except for playful kisses.

He pushed her onto the bed, pressing his body tightly against hers. She moaned. What she wouldn't give to have his body next to hers all the time. With a thought, she stripped their clothes away.

He laughed hoarsely. "I could get used to that."

She smirked. Arching her neck, she bared her throat. He slowly started nibbling down it. She trailed her hands over his body. He gasped as she lightly caressed his balls.

Her breath caught when his hot mouth closed around one of her nipples. Fisting her hands in his hair, she offered her breast for him to feast on. Soon, she was grinding her hips into his. He moved to the other breast. She slid one of her hands down to his cock and stroked. He groaned.

Celeste loved hearing the sounds of his pleasure, and she was thrilled to know she was giving it to him. She wanted Adam to need her for more than just sex. Now that she'd admitted to herself that she loved him, Celeste discovered she longed to hear him say he loved her too.

After pushing away from her, he flipped her over. He pulled her to her hands and knees. He licked her from the back of her neck to the crack in her ass.

She almost cried out when his rough fingers found her clit, rubbing, stroking and tugging. Each move was designed to build the fire higher. She begged him to take her. Adam laughed.

"Soon enough. Be patient, love."

He thrust two fingers deep inside her. She screamed as he brushed the hot spot guaranteed to make her come. He began working her hard, filling her cunt with two, then three fingers. Just before she came, he pulled his fingers out and slammed his cock into her. Shafting her fiercely, he bit the tender spot where her shoulder and neck connected. He reached around to grasp her breasts roughly.

"Come for me, angel." His voice released the desire burning in her. She incinerated, bursting into flames as her body exploded around his cock. Two deep strokes and he joined her. It felt like the force of their climax was creating the universe again. Even in the midst of her orgasm, Celeste remembered to gather the power to her, storing it away for future use.

When the last spurt of his cum had been milked from his cock, he rolled off her. Turning to her side, she grinned at him. "You certainly have a great recipe for relaxing, Montgomery."

Laughing, he tried to catch his breath. "I have a few other ideas we can try once my heartbeat returns to normal."

After Celeste had cleaned them both up, she snuggled close to him, and sighed as he wrapped his arms around her. She never thought she'd enjoy sharing a bed with someone, yet with Adam surrounding her, she felt safe in a way she'd never felt before. She smiled when Adam placed a soft kiss on the nape of her neck.

Celeste let her eyes drift close, allowing sleep to grab her while she grew accustomed to allowing someone else into her personal space.

Chapter Ten

Celeste and Adam stood staring down at the dead girl. She felt the frustration building in Adam. Through centuries of hunting, she had learnt the value of patience. It hurt to watch innocent mortals die, but she knew there had been no way to save this one.

"We knew there was a hockey game last night. Why didn't we keep watch for him?" Adam growled.

"I didn't have any power left, so I wouldn't have been able to track Tomas. There are too many exits and too many people to try and pick him out of a crowd. Plus as far as we knew, Tomas had never killed this close together." Celeste turned away from the empty eyes of the girl.

"Why is he escalating now?" Adam followed her.

"I'm getting closer to him. Before, I had no real way of finding him. I knew he was in Detroit, but I couldn't connect with him."

"Nervous? Why would he be nervous about you?"

Celeste knew it wasn't an insult to her. Adam truly didn't know why Tomas would be afraid of her.

"Celeste is the most powerful of the Enforcers." William appeared beside them.

Adam jumped and Celeste frowned. "You can't just appear, William. This place is crawling with policemen."

William waved his hand. "They all think I arrived with you. Their minds are easily manipulated."

"You can't do that," she said harshly. "You're an Enforcer, William. You aren't supposed to take advantage."

William was obviously unconcerned. "Oh, is that one of the unspoken but deeply understood rules of the Enforcer Creed, Celeste? No one explained them to me. We have powers they have never heard of, so why can't we use them?" William shrugged. "Anyway, it's quicker to do this than follow you around on foot all day. You know how lazy I am, darling."

Celeste shook her head at him. She closed her eyes and shut out all the noise. She linked with William. Touching Adam, she found the lust simmering underneath. She grabbed that and began to search outward across the city to find Tomas.

"Ah, my dear. You found my latest offering." Tomas' touch felt oily to Celeste's mind.

"Another so soon, Tomas? Are you getting worried about us finding you?"

"I have no doubt you will find me in the end, Celeste. The question you must ask yourself is how many will die before you do?"

"If you know I'll find you, why kill them?"

"I told you before, my dear. I kill because I can. These mortals are nothing to us. They are weak creatures, prone to overwhelming emotions. They will never reach our level of perfection. Why do you care for them so much? You didn't when we followed Lucifer down. Did you lose your nerve?" he taunted her.

"It takes more nerve to admit to being wrong. He cares for them. There must be a reason for it."

"You have once again fallen under their spell, Celeste. What do these mortal men have that makes you pant after them like a bitch in heat?"

Celeste knew Tomas would never understand why she enjoyed spending time with mortals. There were times when even she didn't.

"Time's up, love." Tomas' touch disappeared.

"Damn!" Celeste muttered.

"Lose him?" William must have felt the drain on her power when Celeste connected with him.

"Can't you connect with him? He is one of your kind," Adam asked William.

William shook his head. "He's blocking me. Tomas wants Celeste to be the one who finds him, so he's only letting her into his mind. What happened?"

She shrugged. "I'm a little closer to finding him, but he shut me out before I could lock onto him."

"Did he tell you why he's killing these women?" Adam asked.

William raised his eyebrows. "The kind of business you're in and you have to ask why Tomas kills."

"Everyone has their own reasons for ending someone's life."

"The only reason Tomas has is because he can. He kills them so he can feel powerful. These women are nothing to him. Just animals he can slaughter for his own enjoyment." Celeste walked over to one of the police officers. She told them to start searching the southern part of the city.

"I have to head to my office for a while, Celeste. I've been spending too much time on this case. Jakar is getting anxious about some other business," Adam said as she joined them again.

"Okay, I have to go to mine as well. Have to do some work on paying cases. There are people who work for me that depend on their pay cheques." She drew Adam to her.

They wrapped their arms around each other, neither seemed to want to say goodbye, but knowing they both had other things to do at the moment. Celeste brought Adam's mouth to hers, giving him a quick kiss before heading to her car.

* * * *

Adam growled. How had things got out of hand so quickly? Jakar was right. He needed to take a firmer hand on the gang. He walked down the sidewalk. It wasn't the best part of Detroit, but Adam wasn't worried about getting accosted. No one, not even the druggies, were stupid enough to try anything with him.

He had dealt with the idiot trying to hone in on some of his business deals in the east end. The man had really believed the Russians would deal with him instead of Adam. The Russians knew who would get them the best deal and they weren't going to turn their backs on him. Especially since Adam had saved the boss' stupid son from a bunch of gang-bangers earlier that year. He was lost in thought when he heard a whisper from the alley next to him.

"Hey, man. You're Montgomery, right?" a harsh voice came from the dark shadows.

"Yes," Adam said slowly.

The tall, painfully thin man stepping away from the wall didn't seem much of a threat. He had the nervous twitch of a strung-out junkie. "I might have some news about the killer everyone's looking for." The man was unwashed, with long matted hair and dirt crusted clothes. His hands shook, but it was his eyes that caught Adam's attention. A bright gleaming grey, they stared hard at Adam. They were clear of the haze frequent drug users had. Adam had a feeling he had met this man before.

"Why come to me?" Adam started to turn away.

"Come on, man. You know cops. They'll drag me in and make me sit around while they check out the tip." He held out a hand. "I don't have that kind of time. Besides, you're working with the Young woman."

"How do you know her?"

The man shrugged. "The street folks know her. She's looking in the wrong place. Tell her Mike said to check out the area around River Rouge. The folks are starting to avoid it."

Adam handed Mike a hundred. "Maybe you should think about getting clean."

Mike tucked the money in the pocket of his threadbare jeans. "There will always be people like me, Montgomery. They will always need a champion. Make sure you tell the Enforcer."

Before Adam had assimilated what Mike said, the homeless man was gone.

* * * *

Adam strolled into Celeste's office. She glanced up to see the frown gracing his face.

"What's wrong?" Celeste set aside the paper she had been studying.

"Do you know a street person named Mike?"

She shrugged. "I know a lot of street people. Not all of them give me their names. What did he look like?"

Adam closed his eyes. "He was extremely tall and rather mangy looking. He had interesting eyes."

"Eyes?" Celeste couldn't hide her interest.

"Yeah, they were an unusual shade of grey." He glared at her. "So do you know him?"

After standing, Celeste walked to the window. She stared out over Woodward Avenue. Finally she said, "I might know who he is. What did he tell you?"

"You're looking in the wrong place. Things are going down in River Rouge. He said people are beginning to avoid it." Adam moved up behind her. Wrapping his arms around her, he pulled her tight against him. "Who was he, Celeste?"

She sighed. "An old friend."

"How do you know him?"

"Those who live on the streets are closer to Heaven and Hell than you are. They know who I am from the moment we meet. Mike has been on the streets the longest. We've known each other for a long time. Don't go looking for him, Adam. You'll never find him."

"I feel like I've met him before."

"He's that kind of person, I guess." She turned. "Don't worry about him. Do you have someone willing to do a little looking around down in River Rouge?"

"I'll call Jakar and have him send someone. What about William?"

"While William says he's here to help me, he works at his own pace. I can't order him to go anywhere."

"A lot of help he is," Adam mumbled.

"When the time comes, he will be a great deal of help, Adam." She kissed his chin. "I know something we could be doing that's a lot more fun than wondering where William is."

"Do you now? And what would that be?" Adam smiled down at her.

She pulled his head down to whisper in his ear. Laughing, he dragged her out of the office.

* * * *

"Celeste," Adam gasped as she looked up from where she was finishing licking him clean.

She smiled at him. "I think I'm getting addicted to your taste, Montgomery." She lay down beside him, curling into his side.

"I know I'm addicted to you. I just can't do anything about this craving right at the moment. You've worn me out." Adam laughed.

"We really need to work on your stamina." She sighed as Adam ran his fingers through her hair.

As the silence deepened, she moved closer to him, settling her head on his chest and her arm around his waist. He tightened his arms around her then brushed a kiss over her hair.

"I do love you, Celeste," he whispered through the darkness.

She tensed.

"I know you don't want to hear it. Or you think that it's just the fact that you're an angel and I would love you anyway." He took a deep breath. "It's not that. I don't make friends easily. I certainly don't fall in love. But from the first moment I saw you, I knew you were going to make a difference in my life. Of course, I told myself we were just going to have great sex. I was right about that. No one would get out of bed if they had the kind of sex we have."

He could tell his admission had startled and frightened her. For the first time in his life, Adam was thinking about someone else. He wanted to make her happy. He had a feeling his whole life was about to change and only she could determine whether it would be a good or bad change. She started to speak.

"Don't talk. I guess I don't want to hear what I'm pretty sure you're going to tell me. Just let me bask in the glow of love for a while before you destroy all my dreams."

She pushed herself up to lean over him. Touching her lips to his in a soft kiss, she smiled. "I won't say what you seem to think I should. When the time is right, Adam, I will let you know exactly how I feel."

Celeste slid her hand down his body to cup his balls. So she hadn't said that she loved him out loud, but he was willing to believe that her actions were telling him how she really felt.

Chapter Eleven

William stood in the middle of a rundown house in River Rouge. Murderers, druggies and gangs controlled this side of Detroit. He knew that even Adam's Demons stayed out of the area if they could. He saw Celeste's nose wrinkle against the smells pervading the room. The garbage piled in the corners couldn't cover the stains marring the floor.

William knelt down by one, but didn't touch it, feeling a flash of anger. He had never understood the senseless killing of humans that other fallen seemed to enjoy. Maybe that was why he'd chosen to be an Enforcer. Of course, it could have been that it takes a lot of energy to be bad. William knew he was lazy and far more interested in his own comforts than those of the mortals around him, but seeing the blood staining the floor and being able to feel the pain and fear hanging in the room was filling him with rage.

A gentle touch on his shoulder made him look up. Celeste stood over him, and her eyes were filled with tears. They were both reacting to the sadness hanging in the air.

"This place will be haunted from now on," William stated as he straightened then moved towards the window. "We have to find him, Celeste."

"I know, William." She wandered around the room. "This one was strong. She fought him longer than the others did. She marked him."

"Will those injuries help us identify him?" Adam asked.

William shook his head. "No, Tomas will have healed by now. He would feel he could use a little of his energy on healing because he has a huge amount stored from the last killing."

"She didn't injure him that way. This woman marked his mind." Celeste stood in the doorway, her eyes showing that she was far away from the house.

"She would have to be very strong mentally to do that."

"I can feel her. It's like she attached part of her essence to him. It feels almost like a scent." Celeste moved to the sidewalk then glanced up and down the street.

"Which way did he go?" William and Adam followed closely behind her.

"He must have had a car waiting because I don't get a sense of her in either direction." Celeste's eyes were glowing as she turned back to them. William could see she was excited about this breakthrough.

William was excited too. The sooner they could solve this case and put Tomas away, the sooner he could go back to Reno. He missed his apartment and his routine. He missed hitting the casinos for poker. He had a talent for playing cards—it was how he made his living in this time. As a professional poker player, he could travel the world if he wanted to. He also missed the strip joints. He might not want to fall in love with a mortal, but he didn't mind looking.

He felt a twinge of loneliness as he watched Adam wrap Celeste in his arms. It looked like his best friend had found a man to stick by her. Even if Adam still thought she was crazy from time to time, he knew Adam was slowly starting to believe that Celeste was really an angel. He also knew that Adam had finally admitted to himself that he didn't care if Celeste was crazy or not, he was going to love her anyway. William wondered if he would ever find a woman who would love him like that.

"So this link that this woman put on Tomas, do you think you can find it again?" William interrupted the tender scene.

"Yes, now that I know what it feels like, I shouldn't have a problem finding him."

"So when's the next home game?" William led the way to the truck.

"Tomorrow night." Disappointment coloured Adam's voice.

"Tomas will have time to rest and recharge, but it will also give us time to prepare. You two keep pawing each other like teenagers. I have to go and talk to someone."

Celeste laughed. "Who do you have to talk to, William?"

William ignored her question until he pulled up in front of Celeste's office building. As they got out of the car, he said, "I have to talk to Father Michael."

Adam whirled around, but William pulled away before he could say anything.

"How does William know Father Michael?" Adam asked as they entered Celeste's office.

"We know all the religious people in town," Celeste muttered.

"Why?"

"It pays to know the people who pray. So when you need a little extra help and you can't ask for it on your own, you know who to go to."

He noticed the strain on her face. "You should probably rest for a little while. We don't get much sleep at night and I know that using your power or whatever you do has to wear you out."

She nodded. He helped her lay down on the black leather sofa residing in the corner opposite her desk. He took off her shoes and covered her up with an afghan. She murmured something—he assumed she was thanking him. He sat watching her as she fell asleep.

He touched her face gently. She looked like an angel. He laughed. Of course she did. What else would she look like? He had to get out of there. If he didn't, he would be joining her on the couch. It was time to check in at his office anyway.

* * * *

Adam whistled as he strolled into his office. He slapped Jakar on his shoulder, making the demon wince. After flinging his coat onto the couch, he flopped into his chair behind his desk. The momentum of his body caused it to slide across the floor.

"And why are you so happy today?" Jakar handed Adam a whisky.

"Who wouldn't be happy today?" He slugged back the alcohol then handed the glass back to Jakar. "I have a beautiful woman in my bed. We're close to catching the killer. Life is good."

"It will only be good until you find Tomas. Then Celeste will leave you and you'll be an ass to work for," Jakar mumbled.

Damn, the demon was right. Celeste would leave him as soon as she captured Tomas. Even though he knew she cared for him, he didn't know if she loved him enough to stay with him. He was going to have to convince her somehow.

"Jakar, make sure a dozen red roses get delivered to Celeste's apartment this afternoon. Make sure my usual table is reserved at Antonio's. I need a bottle of Cristal chilling at my house tonight."

Jakar laughed. "Trying to bribe her into staying, huh?"

Adam glared at him.

"Yes, sir. I'll make sure everything is taken care of. Now, these business deals need your attention." Jakar placed some contracts in front of Adam.

* * * *

The bouquet of roses was delivered just as William arrived at Celeste's apartment. He laughed at her expression. "I can guess who those are from. He's starting to get nervous now that the end is near. He wants you to realise all that you'll be losing if you leave him."

Celeste didn't look at William. Her heart was racing—she knew what Adam was trying to do. She understood that he needed to tie her to him. By sending her roses and taking her out to a fancy restaurant, he was trying to prove he could take care of her. She was worried about him taking care of her heart. What if he got bored with her? Part of her charm, she knew, was the fact that she had been unavailable for so long. Now that he could fuck her any time he wanted, maybe part of her allure would wear off.

"How do you feel about him, Celeste?" William's quiet question reminded her that he was still in the room.

With a slight smile, she turned to him. "I guess I must love him, William."

"You guess?"

"I can't seem to think of anyone else but him. I enjoy fucking him, but it's more than that. I enjoy just spending time with him no matter what we do. I've never felt this way with any of the mortals I've been with through the centuries." She sat and stared at the floor.

"Maybe even those of us who have fallen from grace have a soul mate out there. Maybe through the years, you've been searching for each other and now He's finally allowed you to be together."

Celeste turned to look at him, her eyebrows raised in surprise.

"Of course, I could just be talking out of my ass. It's probably nothing more than chemistry. You want him. He wants you. Sometimes it isn't any more complicated than that, Celeste. You tend to overthink things." After walking over, William cupped her chin in his hand. When her gaze met his, he smiled at her. "Just enjoy it, Celeste. Let whatever comes, come. Don't hurt yourself before you need to. Maybe you should take the leap that his feelings are real. Let your heart love him, Celeste. Find some peace for both of you."

"What about you, William?" She looked up at the fallen who had been her friend since the rebellion.

"Me? I'll wish you both happiness and go home to Reno. There are hands of poker to be played and strippers to leer at. Maybe if there really is a soul mate out there for me, I'll find her one day." He brushed a gentle kiss over her lips. "Don't worry about me, angel. I'll be fine. Go and make yourself gorgeous for Montgomery."

After soaking in the tub for a half-hour, Celeste dried off before rubbing vanilla lotion over her body. Her skin was flushed and she felt restless. She knew it was because she was anticipating another night of making love with Adam.

"Adam's here," William called.

She glanced at her reflection one last time and whispered, "Knock 'em dead."

Adam's jaw dropped when Celeste entered the living room. William's chuckle barely registered as Adam devoured the woman before him with his gaze.

Her short, red leather skirt had a hip high slit that opened enough to show the lace edging on her thigh high stockings. The sheer white material of her blouse revealed a red camisole top, barely containing her luscious breasts. Red stiletto heels finished the picture. He wasn't sure how long his romantic evening was going to last. He hoped he could make it through dinner.

He wondered at the sadness in Celeste's eyes as she kissed William's cheek. It looked like she was losing her best friend. Smiling gently, William pushed her to him.

"I won't wait up," the Enforcer said.

Adam waited until they got in the limo before he spoke. He took her hand and placed it over his heart.

"Why are you sad, Celeste?"

A tear trickled down her cheek. "I'm not sure I want things to change."

Unsure of what she meant, he said, "If you don't want to see me anymore, Celeste, you don't have to. I'll release you from our deal. I don't want to force you." He wiped the tear from her cheek.

She laughed softly. "It's not our deal. I'm losing William."

Adam couldn't help the small spurt of jealousy running through him. "Is our being together making him unhappy?" He wondered what he could do to change that. He would do anything except give Celeste up.

She shook her head. "No. William is thrilled about us. You're my other half. My soul mate, William called you. Now that I have you, I don't need him to lean on anymore." She stared at their hands clasped together. Tears fell from her eyes and trailed down her face.

Adam couldn't stand to see her sad. Gathering her close, he tucked her head under his chin. He ran his hands up and down her back, murmuring words soothingly to her. "Tell me."

"I didn't know William until the rebellion. As angels we were aware that others of our kind existed, but our sole purpose was to serve Him. We really never paid attention to each other. Then Lucifer brought us self-awareness and we realised there were many of us. After my rebellion and banishment, I thought I would go crazy. My only reason for being had been to worship Him. Without His presence, I was nothing, a void.

"William came to me and made me laugh. He was the one who encouraged me to become an Enforcer and helped me survive. He knew I needed something to do with my life. He's been my brother and my friend. Now, I'm going somewhere he can't go. He's letting go of me so I can fly with you. It feels like I'm losing a piece of myself." She sobbed softly.

Adam quietly informed the limo driver to take them to his house. He knew she wasn't in the mood for a romantic dinner. He held her tightly as she mourned the loss of her friend. When they came to his house, he gathered Celeste into his arms then carried her to his bedroom.

Chapter Twelve

Celeste wasn't sure when they had got to Adam's house. She had been too busy dealing with the pain of having to let William go. She knew she would always love him, but Adam would be the one she would be turning to from now on.

Worn out, she didn't move as Adam started to undress her. A sigh escaped her as he slid her shoes from her feet. He massaged her arches for a few seconds. He glided his hands up her legs to hook in the lace band of her stockings, snagging the delicate silk with his rough fingertips. After he threw the second one across the room, he helped her to sit up.

Celeste didn't object to his harsh jerk tearing her shirt apart. She noticed that his hands were trembling. Looking into his green eyes, she caught glimpses of anger, pain and jealousy. Yet overriding them all was love.

"I didn't mean to hurt you. I'm sad that William is leaving, but it will be all right. I have you to fill the void. I'll share my secrets with you. We'll laugh and love. I choose you, Adam. I'm not your mother. I won't leave you and break your heart."

Celeste didn't know if Adam understood her. She cradled his face in her hands and pressed her lips to his.

There was no finesse in his taking her this time. He ripped his clothes off and covered her. She welcomed him as he thrust into her. He was rough, but she didn't mind. He was the man she loved. Celeste wrapped her arms around him as she rocked into each stroke, doing her best to build their pleasure together. It was only a few minutes before he came violently. She held him in her arms and stroked his back as shudders racked his body.

Shutting his eyes, Adam pulled away from her. He couldn't believe he had taken her like that. Where had his legendary prowess as a lover gone? He'd never been so rough with a lover before. He remembered how frantic he had felt while Celeste had cried. The fear that she would decide to leave him had caused him to panic. He had needed to tie her to him in some way, so he'd picked the most primitive way he could. He'd claimed her with his body.

He brushed her hair from her face. "I'm sorry, angel. I shouldn't have been so rough with you."

Celeste smiled up at him. "It's all right. You have to believe me when I tell you that I don't plan on leaving you. I'll be beside you for as long as you're alive."

"What if I'm like my father? What if I make you leave?" Adam's heart filled with anguish.

Celeste laughed softly. "Darling, I've already had the worst thing happen to me that could possibly happen. I'm not trying to belittle you, but your anger and violence couldn't compare to His. You would never be violent with me anyway. It isn't in you to hurt someone you love."

"I have hurt people. Don't make me out to be some kind of Robin Hood. I don't rob the rich and give to the poor. Sometimes I rob both the rich and the poor." For the first time Adam felt a twinge of guilt when he thought about his past.

"You would never look good in green tights." Celeste shrugged. "You did what you had to do to survive. I don't blame you for it. The streets are a jungle and it's kill or be killed sometimes. People who live in nice houses, drive nice cars and have nice lives can't relate and so they judge you. I've been down about as low as an angel can go, but I've managed to make it and so have you. Now that we have each other, we'll learn how to change together."

"Even if I change, the money we live on will have come from hurting others."

"I've lived for centuries, Adam. I have money. We could give all of yours away and still be well off. Don't over think things. We have to capture Tomas first and then we can worry about how we're going to live." She slid her hands down Adam's back to cup his ass. "Right now, I think we can figure out how to find a small piece of heaven."

Adam laughed as he moved his hips. His cock had got hard again while they'd talked. It seemed Celeste's body just naturally turned him on. He knew he wouldn't be needing Viagra even forty years from then to have her.

* * * *

"*Celeste.*" Tomas' voice echoed in her mind.

Adam's arms were entwined around her, but she travelled to a quiet place in her dreams. *"What do you want, Tomas?"*

The fallen was standing in front of her. His long blond hair was dirty and his black eyes were crazed. The centuries had been hard on him. Madness shone in him, but hidden deep within was a small amount of weariness. Celeste had the feeling that Tomas wanted out of his life and punishment.

He laughed. *"The list is truly endless, but at the top would be peace. I'm tired, Celeste. Too many years living on this hellhole without any hope of change. There have been too many nights with dreams of a place I'll never go back to."*

Celeste felt a touch of sympathy for Tomas. The fallen that turned evil tended to be the ones who suffered the loss of Heaven the most. They were the ones who wanted mortals to suffer along with them. *"Then why don't you end it?"*

"I'm a coward, my friend. I can't kill myself."

"So you're going to let William and I do it for you." Celeste's contempt dripped in her voice.

Tomas shrugged. *"Of course. You both have always been the strongest of the Enforcers. You have lasted longer than any of the others. That is why I started killing. I was going to settle in Detroit and just mind my own business. Then the dreams got worse. There was nothing I could do that would stop them. Finally I decided it was time. You were already here, so I knew it wouldn't be hard to get you to come after me."*

"I'll find you, Tomas, and when I do, there will be no hope of salvation. There have been too many dead women, too many lives snuffed out because you're a coward."

"True, but I knew that when I joined Lucifer's army instead of fighting for the other side. It was easier to get swept up in the emotions than to think for myself." Tomas

shifted restlessly. *"It will be morning soon and your hunt will continue. I look forward to our final meeting."* He bowed his head and disappeared.

Celeste shuddered and Adam pulled her closer to him. Half asleep, Celeste noticed the shining figure that soothed them. Standing in the shadows of the bedroom, Mika'il's silvery grey eyes were filled with compassion and a thinly disguised look of longing. She closed her eyes, not sure whether she'd seen Mika'il or just imagined him there.

* * * *

"He's using us," Celeste informed William as they met in Adam's breakfast nook.

William nodded. "It makes sense. Tomas never was the most courageous of angels. He won't have the strength to kill himself. This way, he dies—or so he thinks—and we're left with the guilt of having dealt with him."

"The ultimate act of selfishness, I guess." Adam sat down next to Celeste. "How do you know what he wants?"

"We connected while I was sleeping." At Adam's eager look, she shook her head. "It was a place out of time. I couldn't get a hint of where he might be. I think our best bet is to go back to Joe Louis today and scout out the entrances. He probably uses the same one every time. It should make it a little easier for us to get a track on him."

William nodded. "You two go and do that. I'll do some more searching around the house we found. I know that someone saw Tomas. I just have to find that person and get them to talk to me."

"What did Father Michael have to say?" Adam asked.

William studied Adam for a minute. "He said that the time has finally arrived. Tomas must be stopped tonight or there will be consequences."

Adam saw Celeste shudder. Jakar had just walked in and his face went white. "Consequences?" Adam asked.

"You don't want to know, Adam. Trust me. When a situation gets out of hand, there are results that are harmful to all of us." Celeste caught Jakar's eyes. There was fear brimming in the demon's face.

"So Father Michael is more than just a priest, huh? Does he have a direct line to God or something?" Adam joked.

Three sets of eyes impaled him. William was the one who answered. "You could say that he is the mouthpiece of God here on earth. Here in Detroit, anyway."

"Like an oracle?"

"Father Michael would be extremely annoyed if he knew you were comparing him to an oracle. He is closer to Him than anyone else because his soul is pure. God gives the priest information that is helpful to us."

"So we can trust what he's telling us to be true." The others nodded. "So, in fact, we've just been issued a deadline of tonight. After that, all bets are off and it's every angel and demon for themselves, right?"

"Yes, and you don't want to be here if that happens." Celeste was finishing her breakfast. "I have to stop by the office to check on my other cases. Adam, I'll meet you at the arena this afternoon. William, we'll catch up with you right around game time. If I can pinpoint the entrance Tomas uses, we'll lie in wait there for him."

"What should I do?" Jakar asked.

Celeste looked at William then back to Jakar. "We have a box of evidence that needs to be planted. When we're done with Tomas, he isn't really going to be able to confess to the killings. So we have to give the police everything they need to make a solid case against Tomas. William will show you the house Tomas murdered one of his victims in. Plant the evidence there. If William comes up with a witness, get him to the police. We have to end it or all hell will break loose."

Jakar nodded. "It'll be done."

* * * *

"This is it. I feel the tag his last victim put on him. He's been here recently." Celeste and Adam were standing outside the east entrance of the arena.

"So if we come here tonight, we should be able to catch him."

Celeste nodded.

"Shouldn't we notify the police? They'll want to be here."

"No, we can't. Things need to be done before the police can have him. William will take care of Tomas."

"But…"

"Don't worry. Tomas will be punished and the police will be able to prove that he was the one doing the killing. If the police try and grab him first, he would never be caught. The police don't have the power needed to capture Tomas. Trust me, Adam. His punishment will be worse than anything mere mortals could think up."

"Will William kill him? Isn't that what he wants?"

"Tomas wants to die, but that won't be his punishment. He would be getting off too easily. I can't talk about what William will do. He is the only one who knows, plus I can't do what he does to punish them. I have never asked him what he does to the fallen he takes." Celeste smiled at him. "We have a couple hours before the game starts. I need to recharge."

A grin crept across Adam's face. "And I have the best way for you to do that." He grabbed her hand, then dragged her to the car.

Chapter Thirteen

"He's here," Celeste said into her microphone.

"Can you feel him?" William's voice came over the earpiece.

"Yes, he isn't trying to shield from me. He knows I'm here. It doesn't seem like he knows that you're around though." Celeste made her way slowly through the crowd, trying not to alert Tomas that she could see him.

"Don't do anything. Wait until we get there," Adam commanded her.

"Damn, he saw me. He's taking off. I'm going after him. Follow me when you can." Celeste pulled the earpiece out and took off after Tomas.

"Shit!" Adam and William chorused.

Celeste was surprised to see that Tomas didn't jump into a car. Maybe he really did want this to be over with. He was leading her down towards the river, away from the busy streets of Detroit. He had a place in mind.

It was dark out, and the farther away they got from the arena, the less people were on the streets. So there was no one to hinder either of them. He didn't try to outrun her as they moved towards the banks of the Detroit River, but he didn't let her catch up.

She wasn't worried about what would happen if she caught up to him. William and Adam were behind her, and she needed William to take care of Tomas.

"Tomas!" she shouted. "Why won't you stop? You know it's over."

He didn't answer her, just skidded around a corner, then continued down a darker street. There was a building at the end of the street, and that seemed to be his destination.

Finally Tomas stopped in the yard of a dilapidated church. He turned to face her as she came through the gate. She studied the fallen. He had lost the glamour that most angels, even the fallen ones, had. She wondered how he had ever convinced any of the women to go with him. He must have used his power to disguise his insanity and general filthiness. She felt a wave of sadness pull at her. She always hated having to end the life of a fellow fallen.

Tomas looked up at the church façade, then laughed softly. "It is only fitting that it ends here on ground that is sacred to Him."

"You led me on a good chase, Tomas," Celeste complimented him.

"Yes, I did." He was smug. Then a frown crossed his face. "Of course, you cheated."

"How exactly did I cheat?"

"You brought Bradford to help you. You knew you couldn't do it alone."

"I didn't ask him to come. He was ordered here."

"Who orders Enforcers around? You're just as leaderless as we are."

"We take our orders from the same person we did when we were angels." Celeste took a step forward. She hoped she could distract him long enough for William and Adam to show up.

"Why would you take orders from Mika'il? He did nothing when we were banished. He does nothing now. We both know if he wished, he could kill me with a wave of his hand."

"Punishing or killing us isn't his job. That's what Enforcers are expected to do."

"Oh, so this is some type of salvation by good works project. How many of your fellow fallen do you have to kill before you can get back into Heaven, Celeste? What happened to salvation by faith alone?"

Celeste took another step forward. She felt a light brush in her mind. William was close. "I have faith in Him, Tomas. But He no longer has faith in me. I turned my back on Him. I was determined to show that angels should hold a dearer spot in His heart than mere mortals. I refused His love. It is only right that He punishes me."

Tomas' eyes gleamed with madness and rage. "We weren't given free will. He expected us to worship Him. He expected us to take those feeble fragile mortals into our hearts. How could I love something inferior to me?"

"So you kill them." She was close enough to him now. She hoped the guys would make an appearance soon.

"Yes, I kill them. In the end, they begged God to save them. He never did. He allowed me to take their lives. If He loved them so much, wouldn't He have stopped me?"

"Maybe He should have, Tomas. But I can guarantee you those women were greeted with open arms when they got to Heaven. They'll be happy there. You and I will never see it again. We deserve our punishment. Those women didn't deserve to die because of your arrogance."

"Arrogance?"

"Yes. The one trait all of the fallen have in common is our belief in our own superiority. That was our one sin. In His eyes, we are all the same."

"That's right, Tomas. If we had realised that before we rebelled, we wouldn't be here now." William stepped from the shadows.

Tomas turned to challenge him. That was the opening Celeste was looking for. She leapt forward, slamming her body into Tomas. Her power wasn't strong enough to hold him without help. Their strength was equal. She would need every advantage she had. She grabbed Tomas' wrist, then tried forcing him to drop the gun he'd pulled. He held too tightly. His lips pulled back in a snarl. After letting go with one hand, he slammed his fist into her face. Her lip split as stars flashed in her eyes and the pain pinwheeled through her head.

She squeezed her hands tighter around his wrist. William and Adam circled, most likely looking for an opening. Tomas slammed his elbow into her face again and her nose broke. She certainly wasn't going to look pretty when this fight was over.

She was trying to refocus when Adam shouted. The shock of the blade as it slid into her stomach startled her. She gasped. Letting go of Tomas' wrist, she wrapped her arms around the wound. Tomas levelled the gun at her. William and Adam were converging, but she knew they wouldn't get there in time. She couldn't stop Tomas. It was taking all of her power to keep from bleeding to death.

The first bullet hit her in the right side of the chest. The second shot hit her in the left side. As she fell, she tossed her power to William. With her power added to his, William surrounded Tomas in a net, capturing him. Tomas cringed.

Adam ran to Celeste. Pulling her into his arms, he whispered to her, "Don't die on me, angel. I need you here."

She touched his cheek. "It's too hard. I miss home."

Tears welled up in his eyes. Shaking his head, he said, "I'll be your home, angel. I'll be your Heaven if you just stay with me."

Celeste turned her head to see William touch Tomas on the forehead. The fallen angel wailed. He fell to his knees sobbing, then his face went slack and his eyes blank. William nodded to her. There might have been sadness in his eyes, Celeste couldn't tell.

The pain swelled. She moaned as Adam's tears washed her cheeks. Looking up, she stared into his green eyes and saw how much he loved her shining in them. She couldn't help but wonder if his love would be enough to block out all her thoughts of Heaven. Was it right for her to force him to become her world?

As she slid into darkness, she heard him whispering over and over, "I love you. Don't leave me."

* * * *

Adam looked up as William walked into the waiting room. The Enforcer's eyes were tired. He had done all the talking when the police had arrived so Adam could go to the hospital with Celeste.

"Anything yet?" William sank onto one of the couches, scrubbing his face roughly.

Adam shook his head. "It's been two hours. They should know something, don't you think?" Adam held out his hand to William. "Thanks for taking care of things for us. I wouldn't have been able to deal with it. Not with Celeste in surgery."

William shook his hand. "Don't mention it. I know Celeste would do the same for me." He waved Adam to the spot next to him. "It may seem bad, but Celeste is tough. She's far tougher than you and I have ever given her credit for. She'll make it out of this just fine. Besides, you can't kill an angel."

Adam groaned. "I might not. I don't think I'll ever be able to forget all that blood. It was ten times worse than when my mother died."

"Like most abused children, I think you knew you had already lost your mother. You knew it was inevitable that your father would kill her. In a way, you were just marking time until he did. This time, you don't want to lose Celeste. You weren't expecting she would get injured." William sighed. "I wish I could tell you this was all a dream. You'll wake up in bed and Celeste will be curled up next to you. For all the power I have, I can't turn back time or change the outcome."

"I know, William. To be honest, maybe dying would be better for her. At least she's not stuck here going crazy."

"Don't ever think that. If she dies, she's in Hell. On earth, she has someone to love her. Celeste is one of the most powerful on earth, and the strongest." William's eyes darkened with love for his friend.

"Aren't those the same thing?"

Shaking his head, William focused on him. "No. She is the strongest amongst us because she's always been willing to risk her heart."

"You aren't?"

"Oh no. I have never been fond of caring for your kind. You mortals are frail and fragile creatures. It's better to use you for power, then walk away. I run from love every chance I get. It's easier to run than to take the chance on losing a part of myself." William stared out into the waiting room, watching people as they talked quietly.

Adam thought about Celeste's hesitation when he'd told her how he felt about her. "I don't know. Maybe she doesn't want to take the chance anymore. She never said she loved me out loud."

"It was a forgone conclusion that Celeste would fall for you. Unlike most of the Enforcers, she has never been able to shut herself off. I know she acts cold and distant at times, but inside she's trying to find a way to keep her heart from breaking. It's more than sex for her. She can't help but fall in love."

"I certainly wasn't looking for a relationship but here I am, wanting to spend my life with a fallen angel who can't even say it back to me." Adam didn't want to think about that right then. "So what's going to happen to Tomas?"

"He'll spend the rest of his mortal life in a mental hospital."

"Mortal life?"

William looked uncomfortable for a moment. "The difference between Celeste and me isn't just that she can give her heart to someone. In addition to being an Enforcer, I'm an Avenger. I'm the one who deals out the punishment to the fallen we capture."

Adam noticed the faraway look that came into William's eyes. He realised William had depths to his soul he would never show to anyone except Celeste. "What does an Avenger do?"

"Tomas is mortal now. I took away his powers. He has become the one thing he hates the most. I created a loop in his mind showing him what he once was and what he now is. Most of the fallen can't deal with it. They tend to go catatonic and thus suffer in silence. Even if they did talk, no one is going to believe they're fallen angels. Most mortals aren't that imaginative." William gave Adam a smirk.

Adam didn't get a chance to say anything else as the surgeon arrived with news about Celeste. Later as he sat, holding her hand, he thought about William's words.

Chapter Fourteen

Adam stood staring down at Celeste. She looked so cold and pale lying in the hospital bed. The machines beeped quietly in the background. The doctors had told him there was no reason why she was still alive. Celeste had taken two bullets at point-blank range in the chest. Tomas had also stabbed her in the stomach. By all laws, she should be dead.

"You can't kill an angel," William's voice came out of the darkness that clung to her room.

"Not even a fallen?" Adam didn't turn from his inspection of her face.

"Not unless they want to die, which might be the reason why she hasn't regained consciousness." William moved closer. His eyes glowed in the shadows. "Of course, if she had a reason to stay, she might come back."

"If she didn't come back, where would she go?"

William shrugged. "To whatever version of Hell she has waiting for her." His voice compelled Adam to look at him. "You might be able to reach her, if you choose to." With those words, he disappeared from the room.

"If I choose to? Why wouldn't I want you to come back to me?" Adam sat down next to her bed. He took her cool hand in his. Tracing her long fingers, he remembered each touch from them. "But is coming back to me the best thing for you?" he whispered. He had seen how the darkness had been stealing into her eyes even in the short time he had known her. As much as she might have loved him, she had a longing for home. He kissed her hand then rested his head against her arm.

He was so tired. He hadn't slept in two days. He had paced the waiting room while she'd been in surgery. He had stayed by her side until the doctors had moved her to a private room. His eyes were dry and gritty. His clothes were rumpled. At least Jakar had brought him some new ones, so he didn't have her blood on his shirt. He closed his eyes, softly whispering a prayer that she would still be alive when he woke up.

* * * *

"Do you really want her to come back to you?" The voice was deep and resonant.

Adam jerked upright. He was standing in a strange room. The walls gleamed a brilliant white. It looked like a waiting room, except there were no chairs. There was only a large desk at one end of the room.

"Are you selfish enough to wish she would return to you? Even though living on earth could drive her mad?" The voice sounded from behind Adam.

Adam whirled around to find an extremely tall man standing behind him. The man was leaning casually against the wall between two windows. His hands were shoved into his pants pockets, but just by the way he held himself, Adam knew the man was ready for anything. The charcoal-grey, three-piece Armani suit was tailored to fit the man's build. The burgundy silk tie and dark blue linen shirt spoke of taste and comfort. The man's radiant grey eyes stared at Adam with searing familiarity. Adam felt like the man knew all of his secrets, especially those held deep in Adam's soul that he never acknowledged, not even to himself.

"Of course I know all your secrets, Adam. That's my job." The man grinned. "Are you going to answer my question?"

"Who are you?"

"You may call me Mika'il."

Adam wanted to ignore the man, but his presence filled Adam's mind until there was no thought of anything else. "No, I don't want Celeste to come back if it means she will suffer. She's had enough pain in her life." His heart clenched. He didn't know what he would do without her, but he wouldn't ask for her to return because of his pain.

"That is a good answer. Come." Mika'il gestured to the window at his right. "Look out and tell me what you see."

Adam didn't argue. He looked out of the window onto a gorgeous English garden with roses and flowers blooming. There was a fountain in the middle. He heard a bird singing. Laughter flowed on the gentle breeze. He watched with hungry eyes as Celeste came into view, holding a bouquet of daisies in her hands. He saw life and vitality shining in her eyes. She sat on a bench, holding out one of her hands for a blue and yellow butterfly to sit on.

"Where is she?" He placed his hand on the windowpane.

"In Limbo, I suppose. She's hanging onto life for some reason, but she won't be able to stay there for long. If she lets go, she'll go to Hell. If she chooses to fight, she could come back to earth and live with you."

Adam watched with Mika'il as Celeste leaned her head back and basked in the sunlight.

"Where would she go if she went to Hell?" he asked.

Mika'il frowned. "That is not something you will ever find out. There can be no other choice. She has given up her place in Heaven. It is either Hell or going back to earth."

Adam remembered the pain and fear welling in Celeste's eyes as he held her while she bled. He could hear her telling him how painful living on earth was for her. "I'll let her have my place."

Mika'il laughed. "Your place? And how do you know there is a place in Heaven for you? You are an unrepentant sinner and have never asked the Father for anything."

"There is always a place in Heaven for those who believe. I have always believed in God. I just didn't think He wanted anything to do with me. I'm asking Him for something now. I'm asking Him to allow Celeste to take my place in Heaven. Let her go there now. She'll never have to endure Hell or earth again."

"You will never hold her in your arms again. You will never feel her lips on yours or her body surrounding you." He gestured to the second window. "Look out and tell me what you see."

Adam looked out of the second window and saw his father. His father was standing there, yelling and hitting just like the night he'd killed Adam's mother.

His father's eyes were wild with anger and hate. Adam couldn't look away. "What is this?"

"This is what you will condemn yourself to if you give up your soul to allow Celeste into Heaven. In Hell, when you die, you will see your father every second of every day for eternity. There will be no turning away. You can't close your eyes. You will watch your father kill your mother over and over. You will watch your mother betray you with her love for your father." Mika'il's eyes held a certain amount of sympathy. "Are you sure your love is strong enough to be willing to face that? It is your own private hell."

Adam shrugged. "I live with it every day. What makes it any different from my life on earth?" He turned to Mika'il. "I'm willing to do it."

"Can you change your life to be a living testament to what Celeste believes in?"

Adam thought about giving up all his power. He would have to leave the Demons. He imagined Celeste standing next to him, a smile on her face. He knew his wealth and prestige meant nothing if she wasn't happy. "Yes, I can."

Mika'il nodded. "So it shall be. It is not my place to deny a prayer or a gift given with love." He reached out to touch Adam's forehead.

"Wait. Who are you really?"

Mika'il's eyes were flooded with all the knowledge of the world. His face hardened until it looked like granite. A grim smile etched itself on his lips. "I am Mika'il. I am the one who branded her."

Adam's world faded to black.

* * * *

"Celeste, come with me." Mika'il stood before her in the garden.

Celeste followed him as he went to the fountain. "What is wrong, sir?"

"You know you cannot stay here. The time has come for you to choose." Mika'il studied her with his ancient eyes.

"There is only pain there, sir. I don't know how much more I can take. I don't want William to have to hunt me down." Celeste felt tears well in her eyes.

"Only pain, Celeste? Look into the water and tell me what you see." Mika'il gestured to the water in the fountain.

Celeste looked and saw Adam. He was laughing with his head thrown back and his green eyes dancing. She saw herself holding his hand as they walked along the street. She remembered that day at the zoo. She had never felt so alive. They had gone back to her apartment and made love like they were on fire for each other. She remembered other moments with him. Other moments where they were laughing, loving or even arguing, but there had always been a feeling of love and trust between them. Trust she knew Adam hadn't ever given to anyone.

"Yes, he trusts you, Celeste. Strange, isn't it? A man like him trusting a woman not to betray him. Yet, here you stand, willing to destroy his trust because of the possibility of a little pain." Mika'il's face was twisted in contempt.

Celeste turned her gaze inward. When had she decided love wasn't worth feeling pain for? When had she lost faith in the very things loving stood for? She was a coward to take that path.

"He prays for you, you know. Right now, beside your bed in the hospital, the man who swore never to ask for anything is asking the Father for something. He's asking for freedom for you."

Celeste smiled slightly at Mika'il. "I will go back. I love him and for as long as he lives, I choose to be with him. When he goes to Heaven, I will accept my Hell."

Mika'il nodded gravely. "You made a good choice, Celeste."

Her world went dark.

Epilogue

"Celeste, get the hell down here or we're going to be late." Adam fidgeted with the cuffs on his tuxedo. He turned to see Jakar smiling. "What are you laughing at, demon?"

Jakar shook his head. "Who would have thought a man who has faced down killers would be nervous about facing a room full of honest citizens?"

"It isn't every day a man like me gets an award for helping the city, Jakar. What the hell were they thinking? Giving me an award like this?" Adam stared at the demon in shock.

In the year since they had got married, Adam had given up his leadership of the Demons and joined Celeste's security agency. He'd also spent a lot of time donating obscene amounts of money to drug rehabilitation centres and children's charities. He had told Celeste that since his wealth had come from drugs, it was only fitting that same wealth was used to help the very people he'd got hooked on them to heal.

"Shows a deplorable lack of judgement, that's for sure." Before Adam could comment, Jakar said, "I'll call for the car."

Adam paced to the bottom of the stairs. "Celeste," he bellowed up the stairs again.

Celeste smiled at the impatience in Adam's voice. She took one last look at the mirror. The full-length black velvet gown clung to her body lovingly. The neck dipped deep in a V to reveal the fullness of her breasts. It displayed the tattoo on her back. She studied it for a moment. It wasn't as vivid as it had been. She thought of Mika'il.

"Go back to your mortal, Celeste. Enjoy the years you have together. I'll be here to welcome you both home when it is time."

Humming to herself, she picked up the little purse that went with her dress, then headed downstairs. Adam stood in silence as he watched her walk towards him. He swept her into his arms to kiss her ardently.

Celeste snaked one arm around his neck, returning his kiss with enthusiasm. She slid her other hand down his chest to the prominent bulge in his pants. Cupping it, she stroked gently. He moaned. Pressing his hips tighter to her, he plundered her mouth.

A cough broke the couple up. His amber eyes twinkling, Jakar stood by the door. "I'm sorry, but the car has arrived."

"Thank you, Jakar." Celeste grinned at him.

"Yeah, thanks." Adam's cheeks were flushed and his breath erratic. "We have to get going or the guest of honour will be late."

"It will take about thirty minutes for us to get to the Opera House, Adam. The limo's pretty roomy." Celeste sauntered out of the door.

"Don't wait up for us, Jakar." Adam rushed out after his love.

"I won't, Montgomery." Jakar shut the door as the limo pulled away.

RENO

Dedication

Thank you to everyone who has ever supported me in
my mad rush to realise a dream.

Chapter One

William Bradford took a peek at the two cards the dealer had given him. Damn, the queen of hearts and the two of spades. Studying his opponents, he wondered if he should try to bluff his way into the pot or just cut his losses. Maybe if he checked, he would get the chance to catch something on the flop.

He knew he could cheat and read their minds to see what kind of hands they had, though he wasn't sure he wanted to do that. There was no way of telling what kind of slime lurked in their brains and just because he could read minds didn't mean he should. There had to be a rule somewhere in the Enforcer code stating 'Thou Shalt Not Cheat'. One of the men raised the pot. He threw his hand in with disgust then pushed back his chair and climbed to his feet.

"I'm calling it a night, guys." He smiled at the men around the table as he gathered his chips.

"The night is still young. You usually don't quit until the sun comes up," one of them said, even though William knew they were thrilled to see him leave.

"I flew in early this morning and came right to the tables. I haven't seen my own bed in a week and I'd like to reacquaint myself with it." He nodded as he left.

Strolling through the Golden Phoenix casino in Reno, William wondered what kind of desperation drove these mortals to gamble away their money and their lives. What flaw was in them that made them long to bet everything on the roll of the dice or the turn of a card? He had seen that moment happen so many times, the moment when the addictive haze cleared and horrified guilt took its place for a while, leaving grown men to weep on street corners with no money and no way to get home.

He used to give them money to help them out before he realised they would go and gamble it away again. Now he did nothing for them. But he was a fallen angel, so maybe he should comfort the most beloved of God's creatures.

Heading to the bar, he wished he could drown his thoughts—unfortunately whisky didn't have any effect on him. The bartender recognised him and had his drink ready for him by the time he sat down.

"Cards not falling your way, Mr Bradford?" Burt, the bartender, asked.

William laughed because, except for that last hand, the cards always fell his way, which explained why he chose to make his living as a poker player. "I'm just tired. I've been busy for the last week and need to catch up on my sleep."

Burt looked slightly surprised and William realised those two sentences were the most he had ever spoken to the man. He shrugged. He didn't like talking to people. The only person he had ever felt the need to spend time with was Celeste, but now that she was attached to that arrogant mortal Adam Montgomery, she didn't need him anymore. Burt seemed to be a good listener, but then wasn't being a good listener a requirement to be a bartender? Burt set another whisky on the counter.

"I'm not done with my first," William pointed out.

"It's not for you." Burt nodded towards the door.

He swung around and felt his lungs deflate as he took in the woman walking towards him.

She was petite, with an hourglass figure he would love to get his hands on. Her amber hair sparkled with burgundy highlights—the colour he'd always envisioned hell fire would be. A black and white bandana kept her hair off a face meant to break a man's heart. Her big brown eyes reminded him of the richest Swiss chocolate. Her creamy skin was flushed and he could feel the anger rolling off her.

Her green T-shirt filled with lush breasts bared her stomach and he caught a hint of glitter at her belly button. As he ran his eyes down her legs, he imagined them wrapped around his waist as he thrust into her. Sweat beaded on his forehead.

Flinging herself down on the stool next to him, she grabbed the whisky and slammed it back. Burt had another shot ready when she set the glass down.

"Slow up a little, Abby," Burt said as the redhead drank the second one back just as fast as the first.

"I swear if the pay wasn't so good, I'd blow this fucking job." She ignored William.

"Thompson do it again?"

"Yeah, he grabbed my ass. He can't believe I'd turn him down. What is it about you gamblers?" Her brown eyes shot knives into William.

He didn't think she was looking for an answer so he kept quiet. Obviously some guy had groped her and it had pissed her off. Standing, he reached into his pocket to pay his tab.

Abby reached out and grabbed his arm, although she wasn't sure why she was talking to the man. His bloodshot blue eyes said he hadn't slept for days. He had all the markings of a professional gambler and was just the kind of man she had always sworn never to get involved with. The hard muscle flexed under her hand as she met his glare.

"I asked you a question."

Burt shook his head and moved down the bar. The stranger raised an eyebrow.

"You did? I thought you were stating a fact. I'm sure you weren't looking for my opinion." His voice came out smooth and lit a fire in her stomach.

It's just the whisky. "You're a professional, always on the lookout for the next game. Do you know the meaning of the word no? Do you force your attentions on women?"

"Darling, no woman I've ever wanted has turned me down." He gave her a slow, bone-melting grin.

No, I'm sure they haven't. Giving him the once-over, Abby found she liked what she saw. By the way he towered over her, he had to be around six-four. A wrinkled blue T-shirt covered bulging chest muscles. His faded jeans were sinfully tight, letting her know that it wasn't just his muscles that were bulging. Scuffed cowboy boots completed the package.

Almost everything about his face shouted angelic perfection, until she met his eyes. Even though they sparkled with blue fire at her thorough inspection, their cynical darkness held a hint of pain. The man beside her had been to hell and was still haunted by his visit.

Angry at her thoughts, she jerked her hand away. "Damn arrogant men. Why do you think that if a woman works in a casino, she must be a whore?"

"I never thought they were." His quiet statement cooled her anger.

She sighed. "I'm sorry. I shouldn't have lit into you like that. It wasn't fair."

"No, you shouldn't have. Just as all women aren't whores, neither are all gamblers arrogant ass pinchers." He threw a bill on the bar then left.

"Great job," she muttered. "Insult the best-looking guy you've seen in forever." Burt came by to grab the money. She saw it was a hundred dollar bill. "Big tipper tonight. He must have come out ahead."

Burt laughed. "Bradford always comes out ahead, girl."

"Bradford? You mean I managed to insult the infamous William Bradford?"

At his nod, she groaned. She was in for it now. If that jerk Thompson didn't report her for slapping him, Bradford surely would for taking an attitude with him. There were few things people knew about William Bradford but one was that he didn't suffer fools, and she had acted like an ass in front of him. Damn her red hair and loose mouth. Someday she might figure out how to keep them from destroying her life.

"This might be my last night here. Especially if Bradford is as pissed off as he sounded."

"Pissed off? Bradford wasn't pissed off. You're thinking too highly of yourself if you think that a man like that will remember or care about anything you've said to him." He chuckled as he pocketed his tip.

Chapter Two

William sighed as he flipped on his back for the fifth time. He had got home two hours ago certain that he would fall asleep the minute his head hit the pillow. His bedroom was dark with no hint of the glaring Reno sun. The images flashing behind his eyelids were becoming twisted nightmares featuring the woman from the bar. An image of Abby lying in a pool of blood exploded in his mind—he couldn't take it anymore.

"Damn, is this a fucking test or something?" He launched out of bed and grabbed his jeans on the way into the living room.

"You really do need to watch your mouth." A melancholy voice came out of the darkness.

He didn't turn to see the man join him. He knew Mika'il would take a seat on the couch in front of the fireplace and that the archangel would be dressed in a pair of tan khakis and a linen dress shirt. He knew because it was how Mika'il always dressed when he came to see him. He looked down at his bare chest and barely zipped jeans. Hell, who cared what the prick thought? He didn't feel like impressing anyone tonight.

"What the hell do you want, sir?" His voice was sarcastic with a hint of respect. It didn't pay to piss off the Father's top man too much.

"What seems to be your problem?" Mika'il leant back and crossed his legs.

"Un-fucking-believable! I'm not even back a full day and you're hounding me. I need to rest, Mika'il. You know what punishing a fallen does to me." He scrubbed his hands through his hair, leaving locks sticking out.

"Sit down. I don't need you pacing."

He flung himself into the nearest chair. He knew he was behaving like a petulant child, but for once, he would have liked to have enjoyed a night's sleep instead of being tormented by the dreams Mika'il sent him. He reluctantly asked, "What do you want?"

"The woman you met tonight... You seemed quite intrigued by her." Mika'il was going to take his own sweet time getting to the point and William knew there were times when the angel enjoyed pushing his buttons.

"Who wouldn't be? With all that sparkling hair and shining spirit, she's a man's wet dream come to life." He was growing hard just thinking about her.

"However true that may be, you aren't a man, so get your head out of your crotch and listen to me. There's something going on around this town and your wet dream is right in the middle of it. I haven't been able to figure out what's happening, but I know you'll need to stick close to her. Also, I think you need to look into a mortal named Thompson. He's been bothering her, and it might have something to do with what's going on around here."

He grinned at the thought of sticking close to Abby.

"Not that close. She's a means to an end, not your next fling." Mika'il's silver eyes flashed with frustration as he frowned.

He didn't care how Mika'il felt. He was tired of doing the archangel's bidding every time he turned around. He was plain tired of his life and the world around him. At times, he wondered whether there was even a reason for him to keep going. Maybe his hell was the endless monotony of centuries of living a life that never changed without hope of redeeming himself.

"You knew the consequences when you chose to rebel. Quit wallowing in your self-pity and listen to me." Annoyance laced Mika'il's voice.

He grinned. "I happen to enjoy wallowing in my self-pity. Why do you think I do it so often?"

"Sometimes I think you do it just to annoy me."

He turned away to hide his smile. "I have so few things worth living for. Maybe annoying you makes my life a little easier to bear."

"You should know by now that annoying me is not making your life easier. Sometimes it ends up making it harder. Now, about Abby."

"I'll find a way to stick close to her. She's a dealer at one of the casinos in the city. Do you think it might be fallens causing the trouble?"

"This whole city reeks of greed and corruption. I'm surprised you can't smell it."

"After living with it for so long, you become immune to it. Reno could be considered a smaller Sin City, so why wouldn't the fallen find their way here?"

"You're right. I think they might have something cooking around here but until I find out for sure, I need you in place to protect her."

"As far as I can tell, she can protect herself." He remembered the anger burning in her eyes.

"Everyone can use someone else looking out for them." The air around Mika'il shimmered as he dissolved into nothingness.

William checked the clock and sighed. He could try to sleep for a couple more hours or he could go and work out. The way he was feeling, lifting weights sounded like the best thing to do. He threw on his gym clothes and headed out, trying to figure out how he could get close to Abby without her thinking he was stalking her.

* * * *

Wiping the sweat from his forehead, William ignored the come-hither looks of the rail-thin blonde on the treadmill. He had spent an hour punishing his body and he still hadn't come up with a good excuse to hang around Abby. The most obvious reason was that he was attracted to her, and while he couldn't deny it even to himself, somehow he knew that admitting that attraction to her would make her run screaming in the opposite direction. It would certainly be a blow to his ego, so he decided the only thing he could do was just hang close to her and hope to be there if and when something happened.

He was walking out of the gym when his cellphone rang. "Bradford," he barked into the phone.

"Hello, Bradford, I'm Dominic LaFontaine. I believe you might have need of my services."

"LaFontaine... From New Orleans, right?"

"Yes." LaFontaine's accent was pure Cajun and he found himself wondering how long the fallen had been in New Orleans. Most fallen angels didn't have any kind of accent because they moved around so much during the centuries.

"Mika'il drop in on you?"

"Yes."

William smiled at the exasperation in the Cajun's voice. "I know the feeling, my friend. Where are you at?"

"I just checked into Circus Circus. I'll never know what possessed my secretary to book a room for me here."

"Maybe she's trying to tell you something. Meet me at Limerick's Pub in the Fitzgerald Casino in an hour."

"See you then." LaFontaine hung up.

William headed home to change and take a shower. He didn't know whether he should be angry or happy that Mika'il had sent reinforcements. He'd never worked with the Cajun Enforcer before, but rumour had it the fallen had a rather *laissez-faire* outlook on the world of mortals. As long as his little corner of the world was free of those fallen that preyed on mortals, LaFontaine subscribed to the theory, 'Let the good times roll.'

* * * *

William walked into Limerick's an hour later. He didn't have to ask for LaFontaine. The tall, masculine man standing amidst a crowd of women had to be the angel he was looking for, plus the aura of barely suppressed power surrounding him marked him as something more than mortal. He caught his attention and gestured to a table. LaFontaine nodded. The women groaned as he said goodbye to them. The Cajun sat down, bourbon in his hand. Dominic LaFontaine owned one of the hottest nightclubs in

New Orleans, The Fallen Angel. His tan linen slacks, red silk shirt and expensive Rolex watch screamed success.

"You are a mugger's dream, LaFontaine." William laughed.

"Do you really think anyone would be dumb enough to rob me?"

"There are mortals dumb enough to do anything, my friend, so it wouldn't surprise me. Are you going to do some gambling while you're in Reno?"

"Why throw money away needlessly? If I want to gamble I will open a new restaurant. What sort of trouble are you having here?"

He settled in and started telling LaFontaine the story.

Dominic leant back. He rubbed his chin as he stared at William. "Why is Mika'il so worried about this woman?"

"I don't know. I asked, but you know Mika'il. He won't tell any of us anything. It's like a game to him. He pops in, orders us around then leaves like nothing happened. He drives me crazy most of the time."

"You don't help matters when you treat him like he is worthless. He is the head of the Host of Heaven. He could destroy us and the Father wouldn't do a thing to stop him."

"I don't respect much. It is obvious from the fact that I am here on Earth rather than in Heaven. Not after asking for forgiveness and not receiving it."

"That's the truth, I'm afraid. We all must not have respected Him to let Lucifer talk us into a stupid stunt like that."

"I'll know better than to let anyone talk me into something like that again. What do we do to keep Abby safe?"

"I'll see what I can find out about Thompson. Maybe there is some information we can use to blackmail him. With guys like him, it will always come down to money. If we hit him in his cheque book, I'm sure we can make him see the error of his ways."

"Do that. I'll try to keep an eye on her tonight." He paid the bill before they walked out of the restaurant.

Chapter Three

The door shut with a satisfying thud and Abby leaned against it with a sigh. It had been another long night of trying to keep Thompson's hands from her ass. Sometimes she wished she wasn't so good at her job. Known as one of the best blackjack dealers in town, the high rollers who came to Reno to gamble requested her often. She enjoyed it most of the time — it was only when men like Thompson thought she'd sleep with them as well as deal for them that she hated it. A picture of William Bradford popped into her mind and she couldn't help comparing the groping octopus to him.

Now there was a man to make a girl sweat. His attitude said he didn't care what others thought of him. She had a feeling that if he asked her out and she said no, he wouldn't hound her for a date. He could have any woman he wanted, so he wouldn't waste his time on one who didn't want him. *Didn't want him?* She smiled. She wasn't fooling herself. She had wanted him the minute she'd run her gaze over that luscious body of his. She had spent last night tossing and turning, dreaming of him kissing her all over. She'd dreamt of his mouth on her nipples and his cock inside her pussy. He did seem perfect — even down to the haunted look in his eyes that no woman could resist. She had seen him at the high stakes poker table that night. He was flawless except that he was a gambler. She had seen a hundred men like him come and go while she dealt. They had an illness that convinced them their luck would change with the next turn of cards or the next roll of the dice. For her father, it had been the next super horse that was going to win a ton of money if he'd only got the right trip around the track. It didn't pay to love a gambling man.

The ringing of the phone was a shrill wake-up call from her daydreams. She stared at it and wondered if, for once, she wouldn't answer it. The insistent ringing carried her back for a moment to childhood. It would start with the phone ringing. Her mother wouldn't answer it then a few days later, they would move again. She wasn't strong enough to ignore it. She lunged for the phone.

"Hello?"

"Hello, Abigail. How are you tonight, darling?" Thompson's oily voice dripped over the line.

"How did you get my number?" She was horrified.

"Money talks and I'm willing to spend a lot on convincing you to go out with me."

"I've told you no a hundred times, Mr Thompson. Why can't you accept the fact that I don't want to date you?" Her voice cracked as the desperation inside her tried to break out.

"I know it's only a matter of time before you quit playing this game. You're playing hard to get and I like that. I'm so used to women throwing their bodies at me because of my money that it's refreshing to have you present a challenge." He sounded so smug she almost gagged.

"Leave me the hell alone." After slamming down the receiver, she quickly unplugged the phone from the wall before he could call back.

Her hands were trembling as she sank onto her couch. She had gone to the police and her boss about the constant touching at the casino, but neither had believed her. Money certainly covered a multitude of sins.

After getting up, she moved slowly into the bathroom. She stripped then stepped under the steaming water. She felt so dirty just talking to him that all she wanted to do was clean up and crawl under the covers. Maybe she would have great dreams to make up for the horrid real world she lived in.

* * * *

"You have to get closer to Abby." With no warning except for a slight cooling of the air, Mika'il popped into William's living room.

"God damn it!" William dropped his glass.

"William," Mika'il warned.

"If you'd stop appearing out of the blue, maybe I wouldn't take His name in vain." He got some paper towels from the kitchen. "What the hell's wrong now?"

"You're not staying close to Abby. I told you she needs protection."

He rocked back on his heels and looked up at the archangel. "Thompson grabbed her before I could do anything. I wasn't close enough. There's a fine line between protection and stalking. I only met the lady three days ago and on that occasion she insulted me. Now I'm supposed to be her best friend. I have a certain reputation in Reno, Mika'il, and being friendly with anyone isn't part of it."

"Get her to deal for you."

He stood and went to pour another drink. "I don't play blackjack. She doesn't deal poker."

"You can win at any stupid card game you play. Why worry about what game it is?"

"If I show up at her table, she'll think I'm stalking her. She's already going through that experience with one rich S-O-B—why wouldn't she assume the same thing with me? I can guarantee that's not the way to win her confidence."

"Figure something out. Things have gotten more dangerous. Thompson called her tonight and it'll only be a matter of time before he gets her address. You need to be with her before that happens."

"Are you going to tell me why this one redhead is so special?"

"You don't need to know. She's worried. You can help her."

Staring out at the lights of Reno, William didn't acknowledge the archangel. Helping mortals was what he had done for centuries, but none of them had affected him like she did. One meeting and he was already dreaming of her, waking up sweaty and hard. His cock was aching with his need to be inside her, but he knew Mika'il wouldn't approve of him seducing her. When had the head of His Host ever approved of any of the fallen angels? He rubbed his chest where the scar had been burned into his flesh. Maybe he would pay a little visit to her house.

* * * *

William stared down at Abby as she lay curled up in the centre of her bed. Her glorious hair was spread over her pillows and he reached out to touch a lock softly. She must have sensed his presence because her eyes popped open and she stared at him in surprise. He waited for the panic and fear to surface but she studied him calmly.

"I was dreaming of you." She smiled.

"Maybe you still are. I heard you had another run-in with Thompson." He didn't move closer. Her light rose scent was making his cock harden and he wanted to bury himself between her thighs.

Sighing, she rolled over onto her back and stared at the ceiling. "Yeah. Someone sold him my phone number."

"I heard about the call as well. How are you feeling about that?" William winced. He sounded like a damn psychologist, but his conversation skills were a little rusty. He didn't normally engage in conversation while in a woman's bedroom. He devoured Abby with his eyes. A light cotton sheet covered her from the breasts down. Her breathing had sped up while he stared at her, causing her hard nipples to push against the sheet.

"I was a little shaky. Why do you care?"

William wondered what she would look like in the throes of passion. Would she be quiet or noisy? Would she eagerly participate or would he have to encourage her? "I guess you can consider me a guardian angel of sorts." He laughed—he never would have thought a fallen would become a guardian.

"An angel? Like Michael or Gabriel?" Her voice held a touch of scepticism.

"Hell no. Not anything like them. I might have been close at one time, but since I fell, I'm just trying to help out when I can." William eased down to sit on the bed.

"Fell? Like the stories about Lucifer and all that?"

"Yes. I'm one of those idiots who decided to rebel with Lucifer. All that got me was banishment from Heaven and an eternity on Earth."

"Right."

"Don't you believe in angels?"

"I'm not sure I believe in God, much less angels."

"It has always amazed me that mortals question His existence. What you believe doesn't matter. He believes in you and that's what counts."

He didn't give her time to react to the phrase 'mortal'. He reached out and rubbed his thumb over her soft lips. Her tongue sneaked out and tasted him. Leaning forward, he pressed his mouth to hers and her soft gasp allowed his tongue entrance. He stroked her tongue again, imitating the far more intimate act he longed to perform with her. Several minutes later, he pulled away. Her eyes opened and she gazed at him. Passion and a hint of disbelief hid in the brown pools.

"This will all be a lovely dream for you tomorrow." He stood then melted into the shadows around her bed.

Chapter Four

The bouquet of two dozen roses arrived the next day. Abby didn't even have to read the card to know who had sent them. When she refused them, the delivery man looked shocked. She was sure not many women refused that kind of overblown display, but she couldn't risk accepting them—it would send the wrong message to Thompson. She shut the door in the man's face.

As she got ready for work, she thought about the vivid dream she'd had the night before. She swore her lips were still tingling from William's kiss. It had been a long time since any guy had turned her on that much, even in a dream. Abby wasn't happy that the first guy she was dreaming about in years played cards. She had made it a point to listen to the gossip the last couple of days ever since her run-in with him—Burt had been right when he'd said William Bradford didn't care what she thought. An incredible poker player, he won far more tournaments than he lost. The Nevada Gaming Commission had investigated him but hadn't been able to find any proof that he was cheating. People whispered that he had the Devil's luck with cards.

He didn't have a steady girlfriend, even though several gorgeous women had been seen with him. Tall, thin model types, without a brain among them, she figured. Of course, he struck her as someone who appreciated beauty for beauty's sake, so maybe he didn't need a smart date. He would never be interested in a small, overly curvy redhead who couldn't keep her mouth under control.

She shook her head. *Get him out of your thoughts, girl,* she reprimanded herself. *He's way out of your league.* But it never hurt to dream, a small voice whispered inside her heart.

* * * *

Abby's good mood disappeared as Thompson took a seat at her table. Her temper was rising, and she didn't acknowledge him. A tap on her shoulder turned her around. One of the casino's couriers handed her a note. Taking a moment, she unfolded it.

Please join me for a drink at Burt's bar after your shift.

It was signed William Bradford. She felt a pair of eyes on her and she knew they weren't Thompson's because she didn't feel slimy. Looking over her shoulder, she saw William standing across the room. Without thinking, she nodded then turned back to deal the first hand. When she had a chance to look again, he was gone.

The next time she checked her watch, her shift was over. "Gentlemen, have a good day."

Her replacement showed up as she gathered her stuff to head for the staff locker room. Thompson followed her and grabbed her arm before she could get to the door. She grimaced as she swung around to face him.

"Did you get my flowers?" Thompson enquired.

"I refused them."

His face flushed. "You refused them?"

"I don't want them. I've told you no. Why can't you just leave me alone?"

He yanked her closer. She smelt the liquor on his breath. "Listen, bitch. I will have you. Don't fight me on this. You'll regret it."

A well-dressed man dumped his drink down the front of Thompson's suit. "Oh, excuse me."

Thompson shoved her aside as he swore. "Damn, idiot. Pay attention to where you're walking."

"I was." His accented voice was quiet, but she caught his words.

She met the man's blue eyes. A look of annoyance flared in them, even as a feeling of safety flowed through her. He moved his head in a slight nod and she realised he had run into Thompson on purpose. While Thompson continued complaining, the stranger gestured to the door leading to the staff hallway.

"I believe you have an appointment."

"Thank you."

"Thank Bradford." He blocked Thompson's grab for her arm. He grinned cruelly down at the smaller man. "Mr Thompson, I have a proposition for you."

She rushed to change her clothes. Even though her arm was aching, she found herself eager to see William.

* * * *

"She'll be here soon."

William turned to see Dominic walking towards him.

"I got her away from him. Why didn't you do something yourself?" Dominic signalled Burt for bourbon.

"I can't. The dealers are told not to get involved with the guests. Their integrity can be in question. Also, I'm known around here."

"Known? In what way?"

"I have phenomenal luck with cards. They aren't sure how I do it, so they keep a close eye on me. If she's seen with me, they might think she's helping me to cheat them out of their money. I don't want the gossips to talk about Abby and me." William sipped his whisky, savouring the slight burn as it slid down his throat.

"I never knew you to worry about what people said or thought."

"I don't, but Thompson would see any interest from me as a challenge to him. I don't want to give him any more reasons to bother her."

"Your woman's here. If you need me again, give me a call." Dominic slapped his shoulder then smiled at Abby as he walked past her.

William waved for Burt to bring a drink for her. She sat next to him with a sigh. Her scent filled his nostrils and his cock was ready to go. He ran his eyes over her body and her lush breasts made his mouth water. How he wanted to take them and taste her pert nipples. He forced himself not to move. He wouldn't touch her. *Ah, hell.* He reached out to place his hand on her firm thigh. Denying his urges had never been something he was good at. He gave her a slight squeeze then started to pull away, but she grabbed it in hers. Her beautiful eyes met his.

"Thank you, Mr Bradford."

"I would have loved to have been the one to save you, but Thompson knows me. He already sees me as a rival at the tables and I don't think it would be good for him to see me with you."

She nodded. "I understand. I wish he would just leave me alone. Why does he want me?"

William stared at her in surprise. "Don't you own a mirror?"

Her cheeks flushed. "Yes, I do. I don't see anything special when I look in it. Just me."

Cupping her chin, he lifted her face to his. His warm breath caressed her lips. "I know a lot of men who would love to have 'just you' in their bed."

He wondered if a man could come just from feeling a woman's breath on his face. A warm rush of heat pooled in his groin. Holy cow, this woman was dangerous. Knowing he couldn't kiss her, he swallowed a groan of disappointment and pulled back.

"Someday," he whispered, "I won't pull away. Will you be ready for it?"

"I'm already dreaming of you. Why wouldn't I be ready for it?"

"A dream is safe. In the real world, things can get out of hand very quickly and you don't strike me as someone who wants to lose control."

She focused on the amber liquid in her glass. "I didn't have a lot of control in the way I was raised. We moved from town to town one step ahead of my dad's bookies and others who wanted a piece of him." Her eyes held a hint of the shame and pain she had felt while she was growing up.

"Why be a dealer if you hate gambling and gamblers that much?"

"Why not? It's the one thing I'm good at. My dad made sure of that. I was dealing for his games when I was eight. He taught me everything he knew and he knew almost every possible way to cheat. You see, I was his ace in the hole and none of the men playing thought an eight-year-old would cheat. So I ensured my dad won those games. It's too bad he didn't stick with the games I dealt. I deal because I can spot cheaters in seconds." Her brown eyes caught his. "I also know how to spot a man who will gamble everything he owns away."

He knew she thought he was that type of player and at one time he had been. Several years ago, when a mortal woman he'd loved had died, he had lost a part of himself for a while. He had thrown money away and made stupid bets while trying to drown himself in alcohol and drugs. Fortunately, they had had no effect on him except to make him sick. Finally Celeste had found him and taken him away to help him deal with his grief. Even though he gambled every night, he didn't have a driving urge anymore. He knew he could walk away from the table whenever he chose to. To humour her, he asked, "How can you know? What kind of signal does he give off?"

"There's a fever in his eyes and it burns brighter the closer he gets to the tables. His smile has a hint of desperation in it and there is a restless energy in him when he's not at the table. He would rather hold cards in his hands than hold his child's hand and unless his child can play poker or blackjack, he doesn't know she's around." Abby's eyes had unfocused and he knew she was looking into her past.

"You're tarring every man with the same brush. Your father was an asshole and you work around some of the weakest people in the world. No wonder you don't have a high opinion of someone who bets a little money."

"A little money? The people I deal for don't bet a little money. They bet entire fortunes. I've watched multimillionaires lose their millions on one turn of the card. I've watched families become destitute because of the gambling disease." Standing, she glared at him. "Yes, these people are weak and I despise them for their weakness."

He let her move away from him. Turning to watch her leave, he asked, "Do you see me as weak, Abby?"

"You gamble, don't you?" She walked out of the bar.

He paid the bill before following her out to her car. He stood in the shadows and watched her climb in. His Harley was parked next to her. She pulled out and headed home, so he strolled to his bike. As he was putting his helmet on, he heard Dominic.

"She has us pegged, my friend."

"Pegged? How?"

"We are weak."

"Speak for yourself. I have never been weak." He flung his leg over the bike.

"You have never been weak? We were all weak the instant Lucifer convinced us that rebellion was the right option."

The emptiness in his mind told him the other Enforcer had shut off communication. He thought about Dominic's theory as he rode swiftly through the night trying to catch up with Abby. The fallen had made a point. If they had all been stronger, Lucifer's rebellion would never have happened. Settling three cars behind her black Mustang, William looked at the lights of the Strip and saw the blur of faces in the crowd. He had chosen to come to Reno so he could get lost in the crowd—he didn't feel like such a freak in the city because there were people stranger than he living here.

"Why do you think I live in New Orleans?" Dominic's voice broke in on his thoughts.

"There are many strange things in the Big Easy. I'm sure you are only one of them."

Their laughter joined together and he felt a twinge of happiness for the first time since he had arrived home from Detroit. Celeste might be caught up in her new life with Adam but there were others out there who could be friends if he allowed it.

"Follow your woman home. I will watch Thompson tonight."

William was about to deny Abby's status as his woman when he realised that was how his heart had been thinking of her since the moment he had met her. What was it about her? It couldn't be love, but it was the hottest case of lust he had ever had. Just thinking about her made him hard. The vibrating engine sent shivers through his body as blood pooled in his groin, causing him to arch his hips a little to rest on the gas tank. *Holy shit.* William would never have thought that riding his bike could get him off. He pulled to the side of the street as Abby drove into her driveway. Using his power, he shielded himself from view, rubbing his cock against the throbbing bike. The pressure started building as he ripped open his jeans and his cock sprang free. After gripping it, he stroked while imagining Abby's luscious red lips wrapped around the shaft. William could almost feel the moist heat of her mouth and the teasing swipes of her tongue. He pumped harder and faster while his hips arched. The explosion came and he spurted over the gas tank of his bike. He took several deep breaths as he allowed his heart to calm down. As he did so, William managed to harness some of the power from his climax. Why had God chosen to allow them to replenish their powers from sex? Why did it seem to be the only effective way of doing so? Some of the fallen believed God was giving them some kind of gift while He had taken everything else away.

Feeling embarrassed, he stuffed his cock back into his jeans and used his shirt to wipe off the tank. He couldn't believe he had done that—it had been centuries since he had used his own hand to get off. There had always been women around who were more than willing to ease him. Abby was taking over his mind and he was finding that he wasn't as attracted to other women as he used to be. She was all he could think about. He wanted her spread out on the floor in front of his fireplace where her hair would match the colour of the flames. The shadows would caress her full breasts and lovingly conceal her pussy. His cock started to get hard again and he groaned. He knew he wouldn't be getting any sleep tonight.

Chapter Five

Abby smiled as William popped into her bedroom, and he was sure she thought she was dreaming about him.

"I'll admit I've never had such vivid dreams before. It's like you're really in the room with me."

He stared down at her and didn't say anything. Hunger was burning in him and the heat of his gaze made her move restlessly under the sheets. His passion flared as his eyes travelled over her body.

"I'll have to remember to thank you, when I see you next, for following me home."

"How do you know I did?"

"I spotted you on the way. You do stick out."

"I couldn't bring you myself but I could ensure you got home without a problem." He sat on the bed, his thigh pressing against her side.

She didn't move as he leant forward to kiss her. He was wondering if it would be as good as their last one. It was better. His tight control over his lust slipped and he was devouring her mouth. A gasp allowing his tongue entrance started a subtle thrust and retreat that soon had her hips arching off the bed. She whimpered.

Somehow he managed to pull away from her but only enough to strip the sheet from her body. With a quick jerk, he ripped her T-shirt from her. Her gasp pushed her breasts up and he feasted on the firm, plump mounds. The noises she made overwhelmed the disapproving voice in his head. He stroked his hands down her sides. Her skin was so satiny soft, he found himself drowning in her body.

He slid down from her nipple to dip his tongue into her belly button. Her head twisted as he moved and licked quickly at her pussy. A soft cry shot through the dark, causing him to smile. Hell, she was hot.

He spread her legs wider and settled on his stomach. He loved the taste of her. No mortal had ever tasted as good on his tongue. Cupping her ass, he lifted her hips to get deeper penetration with his mouth.

He felt her orgasm build. He heard her pleading with him, begging him for release. With one nip of her clit and thrust of his tongue, she came, screaming as the pleasure swamped her. His soft laughter echoed in the dark as she fell asleep.

* * * *

It was still night when William arrived home. He poured a glass of Jameson whiskey then went to his library. There in the glow of a single lamp, he touched the leather binding on one of the books. Milton's *Paradise Lost* had been his favourite book since he had read it when it was first published in 1667. William had spent hours talking to Milton about his loss of Heaven, and what Hell must be like. He hoped he never found out what his *own* Hell would be like.

Sipping the whiskey, he went out of the French doors that opened into his backyard and stared up at the stars in the midnight-black sky. He was feeling lonely tonight. He had kissed Abby on the cheek then left after she had fallen asleep. He had ridden up into the mountains around Reno while he'd tried to bring some semblance of peace to his heart. For the first time in his life, he hadn't wanted to leave after sex. He had ached with the need to bury himself in her wet pussy, but he had left instead. For some reason, she believed he was part of her dream and he wouldn't take pleasure in her body until she knew they were together for real.

Even though Mika'il would frown on their affair, he knew he didn't have the strength to walk away without making love to her. He didn't have that much strength of character — if he had, he wouldn't have had his ass kicked out of Heaven.

He moved to the fireplace and to a picture on the mantel. A pretty blonde smiled at him from the photo. He ran his finger over the glass that covered her face. It had been five years since the last time he had risked his heart — he had given it to a mortal and she had died, sending him into a tailspin of grief. Thank goodness Celeste had been around to pull him back from whatever edge he had been standing on. The love he'd had for Monica had been warm and comfortable — it hadn't been the same burning lust he felt for Abby every time he saw her. Something about the passionate redhead got him hard and aching. From the moment he'd seen her, she had slid into his heart and found a spot for herself. He sighed. This time around, he was afraid it was far more than simple attraction or lust. He was about to lose his heart again.

The phone rang, dragging him from his memories. He answered while pouring another drink. "Hello?"

"Hi, William." Celeste's soothing voice drifted over the phone.

"Hey there, angel. Your husband's allowing you to use the phone?" He settled down into the leather chair facing the fireplace.

She laughed. "Yeah, he let me out of bed finally."

"Darling, that is more information than I needed. How's married life treating you?" He was thrilled that she had called him. The one thing he regretted about Celeste and Adam's relationship was that it didn't leave much room for him. She had been his best friend for centuries and he missed talking to her.

* * * *

He stumbled out of his bedroom. Maybe getting to bed earlier would be a good idea next time. He thought about the two bottles of whiskey he'd emptied after his conversation with Celeste last night. Thank goodness he couldn't get drunk or he wouldn't have been able to move this morning. He wandered into the kitchen and stopped short. Dominic sat at the table calmly drinking coffee and reading the newspaper. He looked over the top of the paper at William's naked body.

"You should really check for visitors before you parade around in all your glory, Bradford." Dominic smiled at his growl. "Grab a cup of coffee. Maybe it will make you more personable this morning."

He went back to his bedroom and threw on a pair of sweat pants then stomped into the kitchen to get the coffee. Slumping in the chair, he glared at Dominic. "If certain people would learn to use the door like mortals, they wouldn't have to see me in all my abundant glory."

Dominic snorted. "Abundant glory? I guess it's all in how you look at it. I did use the door. You have a pretty good security system."

"I meant knock on the door and wait for someone to answer it. Not pick the lock and circumvent the alarm."

Dominic pouted. "I get so few opportunities to practise my burglary skills."

"Were you a thief before you settled in New Orleans?"

"I was at one time. Got some lovely art pieces, all originals."

"What did Mika'il do?"

"When he found out, he made me donate them to museums. That's when I gave up my life of crime. It's no fun when I can't keep what I take." He looked wistful at the thought of the good old days. "Now I'm a solid citizen who pays for everything I buy."

William laughed with him. It was nice to have someone to joke with.

"Abby got home all right, I take it."

He flushed as he thought about his climax outside her house. His mouth watered as he thought of her luscious pussy and passionate moans. "Yeah, she got home just fine."

Dominic studied him through narrowed eyes. "Did you visit her again?"

He stood up to pace as the restlessness settled in. "She thinks it's a dream. So I make sure they're good and wet for her."

"Why waste your time on all this bullshit, Bradford? You can deal with Thompson without my help, no matter what Mika'il thinks. You're totally caught up in her, so seduce her and make her want you. That way you can stay close like he wants and have a little fun while you're at it."

He stopped in front of his sink and stared out of the window. He wasn't seeing the beautiful day or the colourful flowers. He was seeing Abby's smile and her bewitching eyes. "Have you ever been in love? Not the lust that gives us power but bone-deep, happily-ever-after sort of love. The kind of love that destroys you if you lose it."

Dominic's reply was so low he almost missed it. "Yes."

He turned to face the man at his table. Dominic had pulled a picture out from somewhere and was staring at it.

"You know how I feel. I'm afraid I could love her like that. Watching her grow old and die would destroy me. It's better if I keep my distance and not risk my heart that way again." He leaned on his hands and allowed his head to fall forward. "I loved a mortal like that once. I thought I would slip over the edge when she died. What I feel for Abby is so much stronger, I'm terrified of what would happen to me if I lost her."

Dominic sighed. It had the sound of weariness. Running his fingers over the picture, he said, "What if we're here to learn some other lesson?"

"What?"

Dominic's eyes met his. Deep in the blue, he saw a fear that matched his own. "I've been thinking about this for a while. We don't make sense. If God is about forgiveness, why wouldn't He let us back into Heaven? We've repented, we've begged for His forgiveness, we've pleaded for His love and yet for some strange reason He has turned away from us. There is something we're meant to do here."

"We're supposed to keep our brethren from hurting mortals."

Dominic frowned. "There's more to it than that. He doesn't need us to do that. He has His own Host to take care of the ones out of control. We aren't here to keep order. I think we're here to learn something."

"What would that be?" William asked.

"I don't know. What if it's how to love? We've shown how arrogant and selfish we are by choosing to rebel in the first place. Love takes a certain kind of selflessness. We have to be willing to give away a part of ourselves. How do we know we're not supposed to learn how to do that?" Dominic traced his thumb over the woman's image.

"I think that's too simple a solution. We've all fallen in love many times in the centuries since we fell. I think we're here to do more than learn how to love, but I don't know what it is, though. I can't say that I've really thought about it much." William sat down across the table.

Dominic looked up and their eyes met again. "I've thought about a lot of things during the nights when the dreams get so bad I'm scared to go back to sleep. You're right. He must have another purpose for us but I long for love to be the true reason we're still here. How do you do it?"

"Do what?" William rubbed his chest where the cross brand burned.

"How do you become strong enough to lay your heart on the line? When does the joy of loving her overwhelm the risk of losing her?"

"I guess when you get to the point where you know that it would be hell to be without her even though you know that when she dies, you're going to go insane." He smiled ruefully. "I believe I just gave myself some good advice. I hope you listen to it like I'm going to." After standing, William headed for the shower.

* * * *

Picking up the phone, William realised his hands were shaking. When had the thought of asking a woman for a date turned him into a wimp? *Just do it, Bradford,* he ordered. Without thinking about it anymore, he dialled Abby's number.

"Hello?"

"Hi, Abby, this is William Bradford."

"Mr Bradford…how did you get my number?"

"Unlike Thompson, I didn't buy it off anyone, Abby, so don't worry about that. I simply looked it up in the telephone book."

"I forgot that it's listed. I'll have to change that."

"I was going to suggest that. Having it listed makes it too easy for stalkers to get a hold of it. Not that I'm a stalker, of course." He wanted to slap his own face. Could he sound any dumber?

"Of course you're not, but wouldn't any self-respecting stalker try to convince me that he's safe?"

Maybe making a complete idiot of himself was helping her feel better about his call. He could only hope so. "That's true. I guess you'll have to use your good judgement to decide for yourself whether I mean you any harm. Would you honour me with a date?"

He could feel her surprise through the phone line. "Um…"

"You don't have to answer right now. Just think about it and I'll call you in a day or two. I'll give you my number in case you want to put me out of my misery earlier." He rattled off his number then said goodbye. After hanging up, he wiped the sweat from his forehead. He felt like a teenager who'd screwed up asking a girl out for the first time. Maybe he should have approached her in the casino while she was dealing. *Not a good idea*, he thought, if he didn't want to remind her of the main reason why she should say no. He was just going to have to sweat out the next couple of days and hope to hear from her sooner.

Chapter Six

Abby dealt the next hand but she wasn't really thinking about the cards or the bets. She was still in shock over the phone call she'd had earlier that day. William Bradford, one of the most notorious gamblers in Nevada, had asked her out. He was a man used to the finer things in life. She didn't count herself good enough for his taste, and yet he'd chosen to ask her on a date. She could tell he was nervous as he'd babbled on about stalkers. Why would a man like Bradford be nervous about asking her? She couldn't figure that out.

"Maybe he isn't as confident as you would assume," someone said quietly from across the table.

She looked up to see an impeccably dressed man with unusual silver eyes staring at her. She could tell he was a high roller by his tailored Armani suit and the expensive watch flashing from beneath his cuff. He wasn't typically handsome but his strong features and sad eyes made a compelling portrait for any woman to study. His smile seemed to tell her that he knew all of her secrets, and that he still liked her despite them.

"Maybe who isn't as confident as I think?" she asked as she dealt out the next hand.

"The man you were thinking so fiercely about." He bet then leant back. "My name is Micah, and I'm an acquaintance of William Bradford's."

"How do you know it was a man?" She waited for the other players to make their bets, not liking the idea that this man knew who she was and that she was connected in any way with William.

"When I see a frown on a pretty woman's face, I just naturally assume that a man has put it there." He won the hand and without taking his eyes off her, he gathered his chips. "You're trying to decide something about him. Maybe some advice from a stranger would be helpful."

"I don't take advice from strangers." She didn't look at him, though she wondered why she didn't feel uneasy around him. Usually when one of the players paid her too much attention she got nervous but with him, she had a strange feeling of safety.

"I would never hurt you. Indeed, I can't hurt you without severe punishment and I'm not willing to face that." He didn't even pretend to be playing his cards. "William wouldn't hurt you either, not like your father did. All of this means nothing to him." Micah's gesture encompassed the entire casino. "He gambles because he's good at it and it gives him something to do. Bradford has seen a great deal in his life and not all of it has been good. He's had his heart broken many times but he's still willing to reach out and get it broken again. Do you have the courage to do the same?"

She shook her head. She didn't know why she was listening to him but his deep voice seemed to force her to pay attention. "I won't risk my heart on a gambling man. I won't be like my mother."

He laughed. "You could never be like your mother. You're not weak. She never had the backbone to stand up to the charming monster your father was, but William isn't a monster who will steal your heart and break it. He would be there for you if you would let him, as he has been since he learnt about Thompson's obsession with you. Don't let your fear cause you to lose a wonderful chance like this. Even if you don't trust me, trust your instincts and what they are telling you." After gathering his chips, Micah stood. "Trust in your dreams as well, because they're telling you something different than your mind."

A few hours later, Abby couldn't get the conversation out of her mind. She knew what her dreams and instincts were telling her. Her body was more than willing to accept William as a lover, but she wasn't sure she would be able to survive if he ever broke her heart. She thought about the thousands of tears she'd seen her mother cry when her father had broken his latest promise not to gamble. Could she be strong enough to sleep with him, yet not allow him into her heart? She shook her head. Living life was a risk, and it wasn't worth much without knowing how to enjoy it. She was sure that William could show her how to do that.

She would call him when she got home. She was agreeing to more than just a date but she was more than ready to take that step. Her breasts felt heavy and her nipples were hard as she thought of William's rough hands on them. Her underwear got damp as her pussy readied itself for his cock and waiting was going to be difficult.

* * * *

William snatched the phone up on the first ring. *Please let it be Abby.* "Hello?"

"Mr Bradford?" Abby's voice flowed through the phone.

"I had hoped you would call me William if you were calling to accept my proposal for a date." William felt a rush of disappointment. She was going to turn him down and he would die from a permanent hard-on.

"I'm sorry. I'll try to do better when you come to pick me up."

"You're saying yes?"

"You can pick me up around seven tomorrow night. I'd like to go someplace nice."

"Okay, I know just the spot. I'll be there at seven. Wear something sexy. Hell, anything you wear will be sexy. I don't think I'm going to be able to wait." He knew he sounded desperate but he couldn't believe she'd agreed to go out with him.

"Maybe I'll see you in my dreams tonight."

"I doubt it," he said to the silence after the phone call ended. He wasn't going to visit her because he wanted her to be fully aware when he had sex with her. A dream man was nice but the real thing was going to blow her mind. He made reservations.

* * * *

William wiped his palms on his pants. Why was he so nervous? He was just picking her up for a date. Having taken women out for hundreds of years, this shouldn't be anything new. He laughed — who was he trying to kid? She had been different from the moment she had stomped into his life. His cock was achingly hard every second she was around him. As he knocked on her door, he wondered if she would ever let him get close to her.

He knew it was going to be a long night when she greeted him. A pair of slim black pants hugged her hips and her breasts were barely covered by a gold halter-top that bared her belly button ring to glitter in the light. High-heeled sandals brought her closer to his height.

There was no room left for his erection, and since he was trying to be a gentleman, he couldn't adjust himself in front of her. Desire and lust welled inside him until all he could think about was touching her.

He groaned. Reaching out, he pulled her to him. "Slap me later," he growled as he crushed his lips to hers. It wasn't just a kiss — he devoured her and thrust his tongue into her warm mouth. With one hand tilting her head back, he plunged deeper into her. He cupped her ass with his other hand, bringing her closer to him. He rocked his hips against hers.

He came to his senses when he slid his hand between her legs to stroke her. Setting her down, he rested his forehead on hers and tried to calm his breathing. "I wasn't going to kiss you. I swore I'd keep my hands to myself."

Abby laughed. "I wasn't fighting you off."

"You would tempt a saint, love, and I'll never be mistaken for one."

"Let me grab my purse and we can go. I don't want you to get any ideas."

"My head is already filled. I don't want to miss our reservations, so I guess I should get my mind out of your bed."

She whistled softly as they headed to his car. "Nice."

He skimmed his hand over the hood of the BMW Z3 convertible. "I only bring her out to impress my dates."

"She must get a lot of work." She slid in and let him shut the door. Running her hand over the leather, she savoured the silken feel of the fine fabric.

"Lately she's been feeling kind of lonely."

She couldn't believe he hadn't been on some kind of date in the last couple of weeks. "Do you really think I'm gullible enough to believe you haven't been on a date lately?"

His smile flashed. "I've been busy. I was in Detroit last week helping an old friend. Before that I was getting bored with the usual bunch of women I date." He pulled from the kerb and blended into traffic.

"What was wrong with them?"

"Too much of the same thing, I guess. They were nice women with beautiful bodies who knew how to flatter a guy to make him feel important and the sex was great." A frown marred his forehead.

Abby rolled her eyes at the sex statement. It was such a guy thing to say. Of course, he only dated beautiful women, which made her wonder why he had asked her out. "And yet?"

"There was something missing. I finally figured out what. These women could stimulate my cock into wanting them, which isn't very discriminating, but my mind is another story. None of them had anything to talk about, so I tended to be the topic of conversation.

They wanted to know how much money I made, what kind of car I drove and how many houses I had."

She could picture the women he went out with—they would be the ones who grew up with silver spoons and blue blood pedigrees. Abby was pretty sure they were just looking for money. If it came attached to a good-looking man, they wouldn't want to let go of it. She laughed softly. Good thing that she wasn't interested in his money.

"You're different. I've wanted you since I first saw you. You sparkled and you weren't afraid to tell me what you really thought of me. It isn't a pretty picture you have of me but I can understand why. Your father wasn't a shining example of a man. I want to prove to you that not all men who gamble are like him."

She fidgeted as she admitted that she tended to judge people quickly and not give them a second chance. Could there be the slightest hope that he was different from the other men she had known? Maybe that was why she had decided to go out with him. Something about him touched her deep inside her heart.

"What made you decide to go out with me tonight?" The smooth warmth of his voice caused her to clench her thighs as desire washed over her.

"Part of my decision had to do with these dreams I've been having of you." She blushed as he gave her a satisfied smile. Her pussy was starting to get damp. "I want to see if the reality can live up to them."

"You'll have to tell me about them so we can compare." He shifted slightly in his seat. "What's the other reason?"

She brushed her hair back over her shoulder. "You make me feel safe. For some reason, I know you're not going to take advantage of me. My mother gave everything she had to make my dad happy, so I had to watch out for myself. Someone reminded me that I'm not like her and that by going out with you, I'm not giving up everything I am. I can relax with you and know you'll take care of me without seeing me as weak."

He picked up her hand from where it rested on her thigh. Lifting it to his lips, he kissed the knuckles then turned it over to kiss her palm. The tip of his tongue caressed her skin and a shock of electricity raced from that small point to her pussy.

He smiled. Her cheeks were flushed and her breathing had quickened. He could smell the faint hint of her arousal. He longed to be able to stop the car, spread her out on the hood and fuck her. Shaking his head, he sped up. Dinner would be a special kind of torture for him, but he would get through it. He wanted to show her how important she was to him.

"After all your protests about not being seen with me, what made you change your mind?" She stroked his thigh.

He tried to concentrate on her question and not on all the blood pooling in his groin. "A friend reminded me that I could waste an eternity being afraid of losing my heart. I don't know where our relationship will go—maybe it's only a case of lust between us—but I need to explore it. My not wanting Thompson to know about us was just an excuse not to step out on a limb and risk your rejection. My friend reminded me that I can take care of you without worrying about Thompson, so I took the chance. I think it's working out so far. Don't you think?"

She nodded. He groaned as she brushed her fingers against the front of his pants. He spread his legs wider to give her better access. She fondled him through the fabric and gave a slight squeeze. He glanced over to see her smiling at him as his leg twitched. Grabbing her hand from his cock, he grinned at her.

"You're a tease. Now behave—I don't want to get us in an accident on our first date." He intertwined their fingers together and pulled up in front of the restaurant a few minutes later.

* * * *

"Why aren't you gambling tonight?" she asked as he held out her chair for her.

"I didn't feel like it. I would rather spend my night with a beautiful lady instead of a bunch of guys." He ordered drinks for them.

She was surprised—he didn't sound like a guy obsessed with cards. "I thought you played every night?"

He shook his head. "I only do it when I have nothing else to do. I have more than enough money to last me a lifetime. I don't have to bet another hand."

"Then why do you do it?"

"It's a game that takes skill and luck to win at. I've been blessed with both, plus when you've lived as long as I have, there's not much happening that I've never done."

"As long as you? You're not more than thirty-six or thirty-seven." She laughed. There were no wrinkles on his face and no grey in his hair. His body was hard and his muscles were defined. When she met his startling blue eyes, they were weary, full of sorrow and shadows, and she wondered at the pain hiding in them.

"I'm a fallen angel. I've lost all the hope of Heaven and for more centuries than I care to remember, I've wandered this Earth. There have been few mortals I've wanted to become close to over the years because you mortals have an upsetting habit of dying on me." The sorrow became more pronounced in his eyes.

"You're joking, right?" She shook her head in disbelief. "Fallen angels are just old wives' tales, aren't they?"

"I guess since you don't believe in God or angels, believing in fallen ones would be even harder for you. What is your instinct telling you?"

"It's telling me that you're not crazy. My head is telling me to run as far away from you as I can get."

"Which one will you listen to?"

"I'll listen to my instinct. It hasn't led me wrong yet."

"You can chalk it up to a harmless delusion if you want to. I won't hurt you."

"If you're a fallen angel, why aren't you bad or crazy? Didn't the fallen become demons?" She tried to remember what she'd read from the Bible and other legends about the Fall.

"The most stubborn and defiant of us did indeed become demons. There was a small group who came to our senses only after we were banished from Heaven and lost our wings. We petitioned God to forgive us and allow us back, but for reasons known only to Him, He refused us. His archangel came to us with an offer. Mika'il told us there needed to be—for lack of a better word—a police force to stop the fallen from preying on mortals. We would become Enforcers." He rubbed his chest right over his heart. "Those who chose to do that were branded with a cross the demon fallen call the mark of Cain."

"Why would you choose to do that? Why turn on your fellow fallen?"

"Boredom was part of it, and I had no interest in making mortals suffer. I deserved my punishment because it was my arrogance that caused me to rebel. There was a need in me to prove to God that I had changed. All I wanted was a chance to show Him I knew what I did was wrong."

"Did it work?"

He stared at his hands for a moment as a brief flash of sadness raced across his face. "I don't know and I'm not sure I'll ever know if I've proven anything. I gave away the most beautiful thing in the world for a moment of madness and, no matter how much I try, I'll never get it back. Now I do what I can and maybe someday forgiveness will be mine." William took a deep breath and shuddered, seeming to shake off his sorrow. "What a boring topic for you, especially since you don't believe me."

"I didn't say I didn't believe. I'm not sure what to think."

"Would it be easier to think of me as just a gambler? I could be another man destined to hurt you like your father."

"It's too late for that. I have a feeling I know too much about you to ever be able to think of you as a man like him."

Relief shone in his eyes. "Good. I wasn't sure how I was going to prove to you that gambling has no more control over me than any job I would have."

"You being here with me tonight is a step in the right direction, but doesn't being an Enforcer take up all your time?"

"Occasionally it does. I live a normal life until the dreams get too bad and I get a visit from an annoyingly smug archangel who tells me where I have to go next." He paused until the waiter delivered their dinners, then left. "I don't like to see Mika'il."

"Why?"

"He brings back memories of a place I can't see again." William took a bite of his steak and pursed his lips, seeming to think about something. "Did you ever have a place that made you feel safe? At any point in your childhood, was there a place that you would return to — if you could — that protected you?"

"When I was twelve, we lived out in the country. I guess my father thought his creditors wouldn't be able to find him there. There was a huge oak tree in the backyard. When my parents fought, I would climb up into the branches and let the leaves hide me from view. I used to believe that no one could hurt me there and I could dream that my parents loved each other." She felt silly telling him the most precious memory she had.

"If you take those feelings of safety, beauty and love, and multiply them by a million, you might come close to the feelings Heaven gives you. It's the feeling of total acceptance and love that everyone searches for here on Earth. Mika'il brings those memories back to me and it kills me to know that I'll never have that again. It's because of my own arrogance and stupidity that I'm banished from paradise." He looked down at his plate and blinked back the tears she could see welling in his eyes.

Abby sensed someone had stopped next to the table and looked up to find the stranger who had convinced her to go out with William standing there. He laid his hand on William's shoulder as tears filled his own eyes.

"One day, my friend," the man said before he seemed to disappear before her eyes.

"I'm sorry to be so emotional. Some days the pain seems closer to the surface than others. Now, tell me about the places you've lived."

She took the hint and steered the conversation to less emotional topics for the rest of the dinner.

Chapter Seven

They pulled up in front of Abby's house He came around and opened the car door. Staring up at him, she took a deep breath, obviously coming to some kind of decision.

"You'll come in for some coffee, won't you?"

"If I come inside, it won't be coffee I'll be having. We knew your bed was where we were headed when I asked you out."

"I know, but I'm a little nervous now. It isn't every day I ask a fallen angel to fuck me."

"Darling, I won't be fucking you. I'll be making love to you. Let's go inside." With a gentle brush of his fingers over her cheek, he leant down and kissed her. This kiss wasn't as fierce as the one that had started the evening. This one moved slowly and she surrendered to his touch.

They walked up to her door with their arms wrapped around each other. She fumbled with the keys as he rubbed her shoulder with one large, warm hand. She opened the door and gestured for him to go in. He stayed silent as she locked the door behind them and led the way to her bedroom. One step inside her room and he reached for her. Pulling her close to him, he eased his mouth down on hers. They moved their lips together in a sensual dance as their tongues duelled for supremacy. She slid her hands up to thread her fingers through his hair while he moved his down her back to grasp her ass and lift her into him. When their tongues and hips started moving in the same rhythm, he reached up to undo her top. He eased it off her while he enjoyed the sight of her breasts being revealed.

She was enjoying it as well—he could tell from the way her nipples stood at attention. Dipping his head, he blew a quick puff of air over one of them. She gasped and grasped his head tighter. The painful little tug made him smile. He nuzzled and licked her breasts, and little nips with his teeth and quick flicks of his tongue had her moaning his name. His cock swelled and his balls tightened… It was going to be a wonderful night.

William unbuttoned her pants then slipped his hands underneath the waistband to push them and her underwear down at the same time. Kneeling in front of her, he pressed his face to her stomach and stuck his tongue in her belly button. She jumped and gave a squeal. She widened her stance to allow him access to her slick pussy.

Using his thumbs, he parted her lips and blew a warm breath on her clit. He pressed his mouth to the hard button, then her hips began moving in time with his tongue. After sliding his fingers down to her opening, William swirled them around it until they were covered with her juices, then slowly inserted one finger as she arched her hips. She whimpered as he pulled away before working two back in to drum the tips of them against her pussy walls as he suckled her clit. He began to thrust faster and faster until she cried out as she climaxed, then continued to stroke her gently as her breathing slowed and her legs stopped trembling.

William stood before lifting her into his arms. After laying her on the bed, he eased back to stare down at her. Her cheeks were flushed from the passion he had incited in her. She sat up and motioned for him to stand in front of her.

"It's your turn."

He wanted to fall to his knees and thank her. He moved close enough to feel her warmth through the fabric of his pants as she took her time unbuckling his belt. He popped the buttons of his shirt then flung it across the room. She murmured her agreement while she unzipped him. He drew in a sharp breath as her hands grazed his cock.

"Hurry, please."

He caught her smirk before she could hide it—she was enjoying the torment he was feeling. Finally his cock was free and it sprang from the confines of his pants.

"Oh my." She licked her lips as she stroked her hands up and down it.

He found himself whimpering when her warm, moist breath washed over his heated skin. She cradled his balls in her other hand, rubbing and rolling them together. The head of his engorged cock flushed purple when she applied a little squeeze to his balls.

He sighed as she took him into her mouth. She proceeded to devour him, her tongue tracing the veins throbbing along the underside of his shaft. Abby kept her hand wrapped around his cock and moved it in time with her mouth while she searched out the tiny bit of flesh right behind his sac and brushed it. He jumped and groaned. As she pressed it again, he could feel his balls tighten.

He jerked away from her. Pushing her back onto the bed, he covered her with his body as he trailed his fingers up to test her pussy. He found her more than ready. Spreading her, he positioned his cock at her opening, then thrust into her quickly. She cried out as he did it again. Soon he settled into a hard, fast rhythm that drew cries from her each time their groins met. The pressure built until he thought his head would explode. He reached down between them and pinched her clit. Abby cried out his name as she came, and his own climax hit him as her inner muscles milked him hard.

He held her in his arms for several minutes while he waited for his heart to calm. He rolled off her when he had recovered enough strength to do so. She draped her body across his chest. A feeling of contentment washed over him as he ran his fingers through her hair. She was tracing the cross on his chest.

"Did it hurt?"

He wasn't sure if she would understand the truth. "I was already in agony over being banished and having my wings taken from me. The brand was the least of my pain."

"Who took your wings?"

"Mika'il cut them off."

"How horrible."

"It wasn't pleasant but it was less than we deserved. I've always been amazed that God didn't just destroy us."

"How fair is it that He gave humans free will but the moment you exercised some, you were destroyed?"

"What does fair have to do with it? Angels were created to worship Him, not decide for ourselves who should lead. He's shown His mercy by allowing us to live."

"Do you hate Him?"

He laughed harshly. "I can't hate the being that created me. It doesn't matter that I rebelled in a moment of weakness—I still chose to turn my back on Him. He has every right to punish me as He sees fit."

"Do you hate Mika'il?"

"You have to ask the hard questions, don't you?" He thought about it for a few minutes. "I don't think I hate him. I resent him because he has what I long to have back. When he comes to talk to me, I give him a hard time, but I'd miss him if he stopped coming around. I'm a total asshole when he visits. I get the feeling he knows why I treat him that way and gives me some leniency."

"Can you forgive him for taking your wings?" Abby plucked at his nipples.

William's cock stiffened again. Shrugging, he tried to focus on her question. "He was doing what he was told to do and in many ways, I think, it hurt him more than it hurt any of us." He rolled her onto her back and covered her mouth with his. After the kiss built, he pulled back and said, "No more questions. It's all about you and me tonight."

She agreed as he danced his hands down her body to spread her legs apart. He fitted between them like he had been born for her. She seemed to anticipate his first thrust when he flipped her over on her stomach then lifted her to her hands and knees. She groaned as his cock slid into her pussy from behind. William gripped her hips, holding her steady as she thrust back towards him.

"Sweetheart, your pussy is so hot and tight, it fits my cock like a glove," he growled as he rammed into her.

She arched her back and leant down on her elbows to give him a better angle. They both groaned with mounting passion. Suddenly, he leant down and bit the tendon joining her neck and collarbone, causing Abby to sob as she came. Two hard pumps later he joined her.

He wrapped his arms around her waist, then slowly collapsed to his side. Snuggling her close, William stroked her back, trying to soothe her while he caught his breath. Once he thought he could get his legs to work, he slowly eased away from her to climb out of bed.

After finding his way to her bathroom, William cleaned up before he got another cloth to take to Abby. He caught his reflection in the mirror, and paused to stare. There used to be sorrow hidden deep in his gaze, but it didn't seem to be there anymore. Maybe it was simply because he'd just come, and was still riding that high, or maybe it was because he'd found something with Abby he hadn't discovered before.

"Are you all right?" Abby called from the bedroom, and William shook off his introspection.

It didn't matter why the sorrow was gone. All that mattered was that it had disappeared and if Abby was the reason, then keeping her around was good for him. He returned to her, and washed her skin gently. When he'd finished, he tossed the cloth in the direction of the door, then climbed back into bed with her.

Encircling her waist with his arms, he pulled her to his chest then brushed a kiss over her cheek. "Sleep, honey."

She murmured something he didn't understand. William hummed softly under his breath as Abby's breathing slowed. He drifted off shortly after she fell asleep.

* * * *

William stretched as he woke. For the first time since he could remember, he had slept without nightmares. Smiling, he thought about his activities last night, which had ensured he didn't have the bad dreams. He rolled over onto his side to look at Abby while she lay nestled beside him. Brushing his hand over her cheek, he marvelled at the pure innocence he saw in her face. She moaned as he cupped her breast and squeezed. Her nipple hardened and he flicked it with his fingernail. She arched her back as he leant down to engulf her nipple with his mouth and suckled. Abby used her hands to hold him there, encouraging him to continue.

While he teased her breast, William slipped his hand down to her pussy. He was thrilled to feel how wet she was. He ran his fingers through her curls and dipped them between her legs. Stroking down both sides, he was careful not to touch Abby's clit—he wanted to hear her beg before he gave her pleasure. William moved to the other breast as her hold on his hair got tighter. He penetrated her with the tip of one finger and her arch drove it deeper. Smiling to himself, he scraped it against the sensitive walls of her pussy as he pulled it out. She threw back her head and cried out.

Kissing his way down her belly, William wedged himself between her legs—he knew she was fully awake by then. He spread her lips and buried his mouth against her. She screamed as he lapped at her hard clit. While he feasted on her, he slid three fingers into her pussy and stroked them in and out. Her hips bucked while he tried to build the excitement. Abby locked her legs around his shoulders and pressed William's face tighter to her. Right before she exploded, he pulled away. Then he moved up until his cock's head invaded her pussy. One hard thrust in and she came, screaming his name. He continued to pump into her warmth and came undone a moment later, with her massaging his shaft with her muscles.

"What a great way to wake up." She smiled up at him, catching her breath.

"I always thought so." Laughing, William pulled her from the bed, silencing her protest with a kiss. "You have to get ready for work. We've slept most of the day away, I'm afraid."

She frowned when she looked at the clock. "I don't want to go to work now. Not when I have such a delicious man in my bed." She leaned into his arms and gave him a hug.

"I'll be in your bed again tonight, so I think you can handle being away from me for a shift." He swatted her ass and pushed her towards the shower. "Get ready and I'll make you some dinner."

When she came into the kitchen thirty minutes later, he had dinner on the table and coffee poured. She smiled—she'd never had anyone take such good care of her. Digging in, she couldn't believe how good the food tasted.

"Wow, good-looking and an awesome cook. I'm definitely keeping you around."

"Darling, after several centuries, you would think I should know how to cook for myself. I couldn't always go to restaurants." He kept her company while she ate, talking about the different foods he liked to cook.

Once she had finished, she stood up to take her dishes to the sink. Stopping her, he pulled her to the front door. "We have to leave or you'll be late. I'll take care of the dishes later. I'll be around at the end of your shift to pick you up."

"I can take care of myself."

"I know you can, but just humour me. Having gotten you into bed, I'm not willing to let anything to happen to you." He embraced her and she felt the urgency in his grip.

She nodded. "All right, I'll wait for you." She kissed him before they headed for the car.

* * * *

Dominic called him shortly after he'd dropped Abby off at the casino.

"What's up?"

"Are you at full strength?" Dominic's voice was hard.

Damn, it had been a great couple of days without having to think about being an Enforcer. "Yes."

"Good. Meet me down by the river. I have a problem we need to take care of."

"I'll be there." He hung up, bowed his head to pray. He knew that prayer didn't usually work for fallen angels—if it did, they would have all got back into Heaven without any problems. Still, he always prayed before he had to use his powers to punish another of his brethren. Dominic would only have called him if there was a fallen that had to be taken care of.

He made his way to the river. Walking through the thickening dark, he found Dominic standing over a snivelling, dirt-encrusted figure. Dominic looked at him then kicked at the fallen on the ground.

"Get up."

Curling his lip in disgust, William didn't understand how the fallen could let themselves fall apart like that. Maybe it was to do with the madness that haunted their every waking hour. The creature climbed to his feet and cringed before him.

"What did he do, LaFontaine?"

"Does it matter?" Dominic held the man away from him with a grimace.

"In the long run, probably not, but for my own peace of mind, I like to know what they've done." He started to gather his power—he grabbed the threads and wove them together slowly. It could do more damage to him if he hurried.

"He preyed on young boys. He would offer them games and candy. He would become their friend and then he would molest them." Dominic's anger was threatening to take over his control.

Just like mortals, the Enforcers hated those who preyed on the innocence of children. William snarled as he reached out and touched the man's forehead. The man's head snapped back as a silent scream ripped from his throat. William felt the surge of power whip through him as he gripped the fallen's mind in his hands and sucked all memories of Heaven and angelic life from it. The blackened residue of the corrupted angel's power trickled into William's body. He flushed it out into the ground—there was no way he would allow it to stay inside him. As his power swept through the creature, William took the fallen's blood and body apart and rebuilt it as a mortal, removing any hint of angelic power from him. He stripped its mind of everything except what it used to be and what it was now. The man's eyes rolled back into his head and he sagged in Dominic's hands as William slowly removed his touch.

He stepped back as a feeling of depression and disgust flowed through him. The man started to babble incoherently as drool dripped from his chin. Dominic secured his hands and took care not to touch William.

"Go, take a shower, rest and pick up Abby. Forget this night's work for a while."

"I don't ever forget the ones I punish. They haunt my mind just like the thoughts of Heaven do." William rubbed his chest. "Why do we think this is the right thing to do? It's only on the word of Mika'il that we do this."

"Do you think Mika'il would let us do anything that would ultimately harm anyone who didn't deserve it? Sometimes, I think that Mika'il has us deal with it because his anger would be too great and he would end up destroying them all."

"I'm not sure about that. He strikes me as having more control than all of us combined."

Dominic shrugged. "There's a lot we don't know or understand about the archangel. I'll drop this one off at the mental hospital."

Nodding, William headed back to the car, planning to go to his house to shower and scrub off the feeling of guilt that always swamped him after a job. Being tired and very low on power, William'd have to replenish his supply. A small grin graced his face as he thought about working on gathering more power. Making love to Abby would definitely let him enjoy the rest of the night.

* * * *

William was leaning against her car when she got out of work. He gave her a quick kiss, but she could tell his heart wasn't in it.

"It's like having a good-looking watchdog follow me around." She laughed at him, trying to get him to smile at her.

He helped her into the car then climbed in the driver's seat. When she realised they were heading in the opposite direction to her house, she asked, "Where are we going?"

"I'm taking you to my house where I'm going to ravish you all night long."

She couldn't hide the shiver of excitement racing over her body. "Sounds wonderful. I'm your willing captive tonight."

He didn't react to her obvious enjoyment. She reached out to touch his arm and draw his attention to her.

"William, what's wrong?"

"Nothing. I'm just worried about Thompson, that's all."

She shook her head. "I don't think that's the whole thing. Tell me what happened."

"I can't."

"You can't or you won't?"

"Right at this moment, it's both. I had some business to take care of tonight and I don't want to talk about it right now. Please just let me lose myself in you for the rest of the night. Let me take you to Heaven."

"You promise?"

"Yes, I do."

"All right. I'll leave you alone for now. I've always wanted to see Heaven."

"Don't worry, darling. You'll see it long before I'll ever get a chance to return. You won't forget the experience."

He took her home and kept his promise.

Chapter Eight

"I brought a picnic lunch," William announced as she opened the door to him a couple of days later.

"And what are we supposed to do with that?" She didn't wait for him to get inside before she wrapped herself around him and pulled his head down to kiss his lips. He cupped her butt and lifted her up to rub his cock against her pussy. Before they could get arrested for lewd behaviour on her front porch, she broke off the embrace to move back.

He looked stunned. "Well, I had thought about going to the park and listening to the jazz bands, but with a greeting like that, I've changed my mind. Let's stay home."

Laughing, she shook her head. "We haven't spent much time outside since our first date. Let's see if we can act like normal people for a while."

"Normal is overrated," he grumbled as she grabbed her purse and coat. "Have you seen Thompson lately?"

"No, and I'm not complaining about it. Maybe he's gotten the idea that I don't belong to him." She slid her arm through his and looked up at him. "I don't want to talk about him tonight."

"Your wish is my command, my love." He opened the car door for her. As she climbed in, he ran his hand over his hair. He couldn't believe how great the last few days had been—he spent every minute he could with her and found he was wishing there were more minutes in the day. Making sure she was secure, he shut the door and went over to the driver's side. He started the car and put it in drive, then reached out for her hand. She leaned her head back and sighed. "Close your eyes and we'll be there before you know it."

She did as he said and the radio played softly, filling the silence as he drove to the park where the band was performing. He wouldn't bring it up again, but he felt a spurt of fear that Thompson seemed to have disappeared. Dominic hadn't been able to find him either, and the fallen had insisted that he could find anyone. Dropping his guard could result in something happening to her, so he stayed watchful.

"We're here." He helped her out of the car before handing her a blanket for them to sit on.

Leading the way through the crowd, he found a quiet, out-of-the-way spot beneath a tree. She spread the blanket out for them. Before he sat down, he surrounded her with his arms and pulled her tight to him. He wanted to tell her he loved her with all the heart left in him, that she was the Heaven he'd never thought he would see again. He buried his face into her hair and breathed deep. He couldn't remember, but he felt sure that Heaven must have smelt like her—a spicy and sweet scent that could turn him on or soothe him in turns.

Sitting down, he reached out and pulled the basket to him. After opening the bottle of wine, he poured her a glass and offered it to her. She tilted her head to look up at him and smiled. They sipped their wine and ate cheese and crackers while listening to the music. As the sun started to set, he leant back against a tree, pulled her between his thighs and wrapped his arms around her.

"I used to dream about you," she murmured.

"So you said. Were they good dreams?"

"Yes."

"Were you there?"

"Yes."

"What were we doing in your dreams?" A blush rose across her cheeks. He leant down to whisper in her ear, "Were they wet dreams?"

She nodded.

"What did I do to you?"

"You touched me."

"Where?"

"You touched my breasts and my pussy. You used your fingers and your mouth."

Thank goodness they were seated away from the crowd. William used his powers to cloud the minds of the people sitting closest to them, projecting an image of a couple just snuggling, so no one would see what they were doing. He slid his hand down to cup her mound through her jeans, then pressed his fingers against the seam to rub her clit. She gasped and spread her legs a little wider.

"Suck in your stomach," he demanded. When she complied, he unbuttoned her jeans with his other hand. He pulled the zipper down and parted the fabric while continuing to apply alternating pressure to her pussy. She bit back a moan as he moved his hand into the front of her panties. "You're dripping, baby. Are you getting turned on by the thought of all these strangers being able to see you while I fuck you?"

Abby bit her lip, and he could see that while the thought of being surrounded by all these people did excite her, she seemed a bit nervous about anyone seeing them.

"Don't worry. They won't see a thing. I promise." William smiled.

He stood, then pulled her to her feet. Kneeling down, William took her shoes off so he could pull her jeans from her body. He unbuckled his belt and undid his jeans. She wrapped her arms around him as he pushed his clothes to the ground. He lifted her up and she hooked her legs around his hips. Bracing his back against the tree, he slid his hand in between them and stroked her. She gasped and arched her back as she tried to make him rub her harder.

William's heart leapt at her reaction to his touch. The fact that she willingly let him lead their lovemaking, and didn't protest about doing it in public, even though no one could see them, meant a lot to him. It mattered to know she trusted him that much.

"Easy, love. I want to make sure you're ready for me." He plunged two fingers inside her. *Oh yeah, she's wet.* He removed his fingers then placed his cock at her opening before lowering her onto his shaft. They both groaned as he thrust deep into her. He helped her ride him fast then slow until he wanted to beg for mercy.

Abby bit her lip, and William figured she was trying to stay quiet to keep the people around them from hearing her. Her head was thrown back and her hair caressed his thighs. Her pussy started contracting as her orgasm hit her. She leant forward and bit his shoulder, probably to stop the scream in her throat. The feel of her teeth on his skin drove him over the edge as his balls tightened. His hot cum filled her as he thrust into her.

She slowly loosened her legs and slid down his hips to touch the ground. He lowered her, holding on until he knew for sure she could stand on her own, then pulled his pants up and zipped them before reaching for her jeans. She was flushed with her pleasure and he wondered if some of it was from the embarrassment of having sex in public. He helped her dress, repacked the basket then grabbed the blanket. They walked to his car with their arms around each other.

William drove them home, then tucked her into bed. He brushed a kiss over her cheek. "I'll join you in a few minutes."

Moving through the darkness of her kitchen, he found a bottle of whiskey in a cupboard, then poured himself a glass.

"No glass for a friend?" Mika'il emerged from the shadows to join William at the table.

William picked up another glass without saying anything to the angel. They sat drinking in the silence until William sighed.

"Are you here to yell at me?"

Mika'il looked surprised. "Why would I do that?"

Waving back towards the bedroom, he said, "I'm sure this isn't what you were thinking when you said I should get close to her."

"Maybe not, but it's working, so I'm not going to complain." The angel stared down at his glass. "I won't deny you pleasure. It seems to me the Father wanted you to enjoy sex or else He wouldn't have made your powers dependent on it."

"I never thought of it that way."

"Of course you didn't because you were too busy being bitter and angry about what kind of life you had. He may have banished you, but He hasn't forgotten you. I truly believe you're here to learn something and I've got a feeling you're getting close to figuring it out." Mika'il slugged back the whiskey then started gasping. William thumped him on the back. "I can never get used to this stuff."

"I would hope not. It wouldn't do for God's warrior angel to get used to alcohol and drinking. People might start thinking you're like them. You need to project a capable and unswerving image. No one would want to be reminded of themselves like that." William sipped from his glass. "I drink this stuff, but it does nothing for me."

"Then why drink it?"

He looked out into the shadows beyond the window. "I don't know. Maybe it makes me feel a little more human. There are times when I feel so alien in this world and these people. I guess I thought being able to drink would help me fit in a little more."

"You are different. You are neither angelic nor mortal and you never will be." Mika'il touched his shoulder. "I wish I could make it different for you, but I can't. I hope you eventually realise that what I do, I do to help you—or at least try to help. I know it doesn't always work out and I'm sorry for that. Sometimes it does, like with Celeste and Adam, and I'm happy for a while."

"William, who are you talking to?" Abby's voice came from the bedroom.

"No one, sweetheart." He nodded at Mika'il. He felt a little closer to the archangel after the late night confession. He stood up and headed back to bed.

* * * *

Abby's body was humming in anticipation of William's loving. It had been a long, boring shift and she just wanted to get home. She had tried calling his cell to let him know she was getting out early, but he hadn't answered. She didn't want to waste time waiting to get a hold of him. Nothing was going to happen—Thompson hadn't been around for several days now and she was convinced he had given up on her.

She smiled, remembering the teasing she had got from some of the other dealers about dating William. The women had asked her if he was as great a lover as rumour reported him to be. Laughing, she'd told them she didn't want to make them jealous. The men had made snide comments about her holding out for a rich man. She just shrugged those remarks away—she had turned down most of the men who'd asked her out while she worked at the casino. She had a feeling if William lost all his money, she would still be happy dating him.

She was reaching out to unlock her car when an arm wrapped around her neck and jerked her away from the vehicle. She tried to scream but a large, greasy hand covered her mouth. Her assailant pulled her into the shadows. Pushing her to the ground, he blocked any route of escape for her. The fear was almost overwhelming—she knew William would be coming to get her but she didn't know if he would be in time.

The man reached down then grabbed her arm to yank her up on her feet. She gasped at the pain. A fist connected with her cheek. God, she should have waited for William like he asked but she had been confident she could handle anything.

"Thompson said to tell you to stop seeing Bradford or your punishment will be worse."

Worse than this? She wondered how that could be possible as she focused on the burning sensation coming from her arm. The man had forced it up behind her back. The pain became more intense as he jerked it even higher. She cried out, wanting to beg him to stop but her pride wouldn't let her do that. The man was ripped away from her at the moment that she was sure her arm would break.

She fell to the ground, clutching her arm to her body. William stood over her with his blue eyes blazing. His arm was outstretched and pointing towards her attacker who was dangling a foot or two off the concrete. The man's face turned purple and he clawed at his throat as William made a fist. She knew she had to do something or he would kill the man. She climbed to her feet. Touching his arm, she spoke.

"Don't do it, William. He isn't worth it. Let the police take care of him."

William's face was ravaged by fear and anger. "He hurt you."

"He was supposed to. Thompson sent him to warn me. He said I had to stop seeing you or my punishment would be worse." With a weak smile, she shrugged. "Right now I can't think what worse might be."

William growled as the man turned an alarming shade of blue.

"Please. I need to get to the hospital. I think something's wrong with my arm." She wrapped her good hand around his forearm. Feeling dizzy, she knew the pain was starting to overwhelm her.

Dominic appeared out of nowhere. "I'll take care of him. You take Abby to the hospital."

William opened his fist and the man dropped to the ground with a thud. He lay there gasping like an air-deprived fish. She watched as William caught Dominic's eye and the Cajun nodded. Seemingly satisfied that the man would be taken care of the right way, he gathered her in his arms and carried her to her car. Her purse and keys had fallen to the pavement when the man had grabbed her. He picked them up and got her settled before climbing in.

She wondered why he wasn't talking. Why hadn't he given her a hug or comforted her? She was feeling shaky and weepy. At a stoplight, he turned to look at her and she saw the rage still simmered—he was fighting the urge to go back and inflict damage on her assailant. She reached out and took his hand in hers. His grip tightened until she wanted to beg him to let go. He took a deep breath and loosened his hold.

"What the hell were you doing out there?"

She knew he was trying not to yell at her and appreciated the effort it was taking. "I got out of work early and thought I'd head home."

"Why didn't you wait for me? You knew I would be here to get you. Why didn't you at least call me?"

"I tried calling but you didn't answer. I didn't think there would be a problem. We haven't seen or heard from Thompson in days. I figured he had given up."

"Thompson has gone to ground. If a stalker disappears, you have to take precautions because that's when they usually escalate into violence. I don't want anything to happen to you, Abby. You're too important to me. I'd go crazy if you were seriously hurt or killed."

Abby could see his hands shaking from the let-down of adrenaline, and knew it was fear for her that caused this strong man to shake like a child. She lifted the hand holding hers to her mouth, then whispered a kiss across his knuckles.

"I'm sorry, William. I promise not to take chances anymore."

He accepted her apology as they pulled up to the emergency room.

* * * *

William stood on the deck at Abby's house. She was tucked in and sleeping off the painkillers the doctor had given her. He sent a short prayer thanking the Father that he had got to her before the man could do something more than sprain her arm. He had never felt the rage that had swamped him when he saw her attacker hitting her. If it hadn't been for her stopping him, he probably would have killed the man and he wouldn't have felt bad about doing it, either. The man was slime who got off on hurting women—the world would have been a better place without him. He wondered what Dominic had done to him.

He stared out at the sparkling lights that twirled and spun on the facades of the casinos. They soothed his restless feelings. He'd never been able to explain to Celeste what he liked most about Reno—maybe it was to do with the gambling and the chance to alter his life with one turn of a card. From the moment he'd arrived in the city, he'd felt more alive than anywhere else. His heart beat to the rhythm of the clanging slots.

His blood pounded as jackpots were won and shouts were heard. He was an addict and Reno was his drug of choice. There was no way he would ever leave now that Abby was there with him.

"You really love this city, don't you?" Dominic appeared beside him.

"Don't you feel the same about New Orleans?"

Shaking his head, Dominic took in the bright lights. "It's a place to lay my head. The city doesn't call my heart back."

"Then why stay?"

"My heart has found a home with someone who lives there. As long as she's there, I'll be staying. It isn't a bad town. The people feel the same overwhelming sense of desperation you have here."

"Does it make you feel alive?"

"She makes me feel alive. I don't need a city or flashing lights to make me *feel*. Now that you've found Abby, you know what I'm talking about. You don't need to place another bet or spend another moment in a casino because nothing holds a candle to her laugh or her smile. She's your new addiction." Dominic smiled at him. "Quit looking out at the lights. Go inside and stare at that wonderful woman. She will be your entire world and that's the way it should be."

William held out his hand and Dominic shook it.

"I'll be watching your back. We'll find Thompson and stop his threat towards her. Then I'm heading home to straighten out my own world."

Heading inside, William thought about what Dominic had said. He realised he hadn't wanted to go to the casino in days. His time was filled with thoughts of her and wanting to be with her, instead of the men he used to spend every night with. He slid into the bedroom quietly so he didn't wake her. The bed was empty and water was running in the shower. He smiled as he stripped and headed to the bathroom.

Abby's curves were silhouetted against the shower curtain. He made a noise to let her know that he was in the room with her — she would be jumpy for a little while because of the attack and he didn't want to scare her. She stuck her head around the edge of the curtain. Her eyes widened as she saw him standing there naked. Her smile was seduction personified as she crooked her finger at him to join her.

The moist warmth enveloped his body as William stepped in and reached for her. He was careful not to jar her arm, pulling her tight to his body. His cock rubbed against her soft belly. Easing her feet apart, he knelt in front of her. She ran her hands through his wet hair and leant back against the shower wall while he buried his face in her pussy. He feasted on her with each stroke of his tongue and thrust of his fingers. Her hips moved slowly at first as she enjoyed the way he savoured her. Then, as the excitement built, her hips started to buck faster. He loved the taste and scent of her passion, and nothing moved him as much as when she finally let go. Her grip on his hair strengthened until it almost hurt as he forced Abby tighter to his mouth. He was going to drag her orgasm out for as long as he could. When she went limp in his arms, he gently soothed her. After standing, he soaped her down.

Once he'd turned off the water, he lifted her onto the bath mat before grabbing a towel. He took his time and dried her off with teasing touches on her sensitive nipples and tender clit. Soon she was flushed and moist again. He led her back to her bed, more than ready to fuck her.

Abby pushed him down on the edge of the bed. Leaning back on his hands, William spread his thighs wide to allow her to kneel in front of him. She ran her hands up and across his legs, obviously enjoying the rough hair against her palms. He watched her through narrowed eyes. Bending her head, she blew a warm breath across the head of his cock, making him jump. As Abby laughed, she cupped his balls and began rubbing them as she committed quick licks on his cock. She dipped her head low as she suckled his balls and ran her fingers over the sensitive patch of skin behind them. Her eyes closed as his cock slid into her mouth. He burrowed his hands into her hair. He resisted the urge to fuck her mouth and direct her blow job.

She took him deeper into her throat. Abby wrapped her hand around his cock and moved up and down in time with her head. His balls tightened and his climax pooled at the base of his spine. He knew he was going to come soon. When the pressure was almost too much, he grabbed her around the waist and lifted her to straddle his hips. She braced herself on his shoulders and he lowered her onto his shaft. They both groaned as he plunged deep into her pussy. She rode him fast and hard. Watching her, he saw her face start to flush as her orgasm raced to shatter her.

She cried out as William separated them before he flipped her onto her back and followed her down. Thrusting harder, he crushed his lips to hers. There was urgency to his movements—he was trying to erase all the fear and rage he had felt while she was being attacked.

"Look at me when you come, Abby."

Her melted-chocolate eyes opened and pinned him. The passion and excitement in their depths turned him on even more. Her inner muscles clenched tight on his cock. They exploded together, spiralling down back to where he collapsed on her.

She rubbed his back as they recovered. "Do you feel better now?" Her voice was husky with residual passion.

He chuckled as he drew out of her then flopped to the bed beside her. "No, not really. I still blame myself for not being there to protect you."

"You didn't know I was getting out early. How could you have been there?"

"I can do a lot of things you don't know about." He saw her grimace as she pulled a blanket over them. He took her injured arm in his hands. "Is your arm okay? I'm sorry I forgot about it. Obviously I was thinking with my other head."

Abby smiled weakly.

"It only hurts a little." She gasped as a dim blue light came from William's hands to engulf her arm. "What was that?"

"I can do a limited amount of healing when I'm at full strength." He pulled her into his arms and tucked her head under his chin. "Enough to take away most of the pain."

"What do you mean, at full strength?"

"God may have taken our wings but He gave us other powers to help keep our brethren in line—all of the Enforcers have different kinds of power. We're stronger than most mortals, and I can disappear and reappear in a different spot. Aside from being an Enforcer, I'm also an Avenger."

"What's that?" Abby asked.

Rubbing his chin against her soft hair, William was quiet for a moment. "When a fallen has been captured by an Enforcer, I'm one of a few who will be called in to punish the evil one. I take away all his power and make him mortal."

"That isn't so bad."

"Honey, to a fallen who has been a superior being since his creation, becoming mortal is a death sentence. They have no way of coping with real life. Most of them become catatonic and spend the rest of their lives in mental hospitals." A hint of sadness sounded in his voice. "It takes me a while to get over the guilt when I do something like that."

"Guilt?"

"It isn't always right to punish someone for lashing out in anger. The demon fallen are angry and jealous over the love God has for mortals. Some of them were never able to deal with their banishment. They are the ones who let the anger get out of control. That's when I step in and stop them. I don't always think it's right, but thinking is what got me into trouble in the first place."

"How do you get your power?"

"That's the most enjoyable part. Every time we have sex, I get power. Each orgasm and climax releases energy that I can use. I store it away until I need it. I was able to heal you because I'm at full power now."

"Isn't that convenient?"

He could hear the sarcasm in her voice. "Maybe in a small way, God is making up for our punishment. We're able to get some joy out of life."

"I certainly enjoy the methods you employ to gather your power."

"I do too, and it hasn't been so much fun in years. Being with you is definitely ensuring that I'm at full power all the time."

"All the time, huh?" She slid her hand down his belly to stroke his hardening cock.

"All the time, sweetheart." He rolled over and proved it to her.

Chapter Nine

"We have a problem." Dominic sat down at the poker table next to him.

"What sort of problem?" William folded his hand and looked at Dominic.

"I've been looking for Thompson since Abby's attack. I can't find him anywhere. It's like he's fallen off the face of the Earth." The Cajun checked his cards then bet.

"So we should assume he's still around and lurking somewhere. He's waiting for another chance at her."

"More than likely, but there are rumours going around in certain sections of the town. The story is that a true demon has gotten hold of a mortal and is trying to take him over." Dominic placed another bet.

"Shit. That's the one thing we don't need right now. I should be out looking for the demon but I can't leave her. There's no telling what Thompson might do if given the opportunity." He slapped the table in irritation.

"That's what I'm here for. This situation is probably the reason why Mika'il has been so agitated lately.

Damn, the guy got me on the river. I hate playing poker." Dominic threw his hand in.

"If that's what he suspected was happening, why didn't he just say so? Why would he say she was in the middle of it?" A thought hit him and he turned to Dominic. "So a true demon is trying to take Thompson over?"

"It's possible. I'll keep looking. He has to show up somewhere and when he does, I'll be there."

William grabbed his chips. "I'm cashing in and heading over to her table. It's almost time for her shift to be over with." He slapped Dominic on the shoulder. "Good luck."

Dominic grunted and waved him away.

William made his way to the blackjack tables knowing the security cameras followed his progress through the crowd. The management had watched him since the first game he'd played at the Golden Phoenix—they couldn't figure out how he won so often without cheating. He could imagine their horror if Dominic started playing there as well—the two of them would break the bank in minutes.

He noticed one of the security guards standing by Abby's table—word had finally reached her supervisors that she was seeing him, so they would be keeping a close eye on her. He had told her earlier if they started harassing her, he would take care of it. She'd got an independent gleam in her eye and told him in no uncertain terms that she would take care of the problem, and that she didn't need him to take over her life. He had no interest in arguing with her, so he had agreed. What she didn't know wouldn't hurt her.

After Abby had got off her shift, she'd gone to change out of her uniform, plus grab her purse. When she walked out of the employee's door, William was waiting for her. She flung herself into his arms and kissed him. He picked her up and whirled her around. Abby had never had a man so casual about carrying her, and admitted to herself that his strength was a bonus, especially when they couldn't make it to the bed and he just had to be inside her — he would lift her and take her against the wall.

"Why do you carry me around so much?"

"I like you close to my heart."

His answer melted her heart and she laid her head on his chest where she could hear his heartbeat. It stuttered then picked up speed. She realised he was reacting to her being close to him. Looping her arms around his neck, she didn't let him set her down. He looked at her and she saw the yearning in his eyes. It wasn't just sex he wanted from her, and she was afraid to face what else he might want.

Could Abby take the chance that William wouldn't break her heart? Was it possible to believe that he loved her? God, she wasn't good enough for him and once he figured that out, he'd leave her. How would she survive it? She was beginning to be swallowed up by him. She had watched her mother live as a shadow that only came alive when her father came home. Panic swelled in her. He almost dropped her when she pushed against his chest.

"I need to be alone." She dug in her purse for her keys.

"Wrong answer. I'm not leaving you alone until we know for sure where Thompson is."

"He isn't here anymore. He's probably moved to Vegas. I need time away from you, William. You've totally overwhelmed my life. I should have known that would happen when I said yes to you."

"I'm not trying to take over your life. If I wanted to, I could do it without a word of protest from you. You're running scared and it doesn't suit you."

"Doesn't suit me? How do you know what suits me and what doesn't? I'm the only one who does and you can't make decisions for me. You're starting to overwhelm me, and I don't want to be just an extension of your will."

"What decision have I tried to make for you? What's wrong?"

"You're crowding me. I can't breathe and I need time to think about everything. So please, leave me alone tonight."

He stepped back and glared at her. "Okay, I'll follow you home." He held up a hand to stop her protest. "I didn't say I would stay. I'm following you home to make sure no one else does and then I'll leave you alone. Thompson isn't gone and I'm afraid he's waiting for another moment like this one."

She didn't say goodbye as she climbed into her car. In her rear-view mirror, she saw him standing in the same spot she had left him in. How was he going to follow her home if he let her get that far ahead of him? It didn't matter right then—all that mattered was the need she had to get away from him and think. Abby concentrated on driving until she pulled into her driveway. She unlocked her front door and turned to see William drive off.

She couldn't believe the sense of sadness and loneliness she felt knowing she wouldn't be sleeping in his arms that night. As she moved through her house, she realised just how much he had become a part of her life. She could smell a faint hint of his cologne throughout the rooms. In her kitchen, the coffee mug he always used was sitting on the counter where he had left it that morning. The novel he was in the middle of reading lay face down on her coffee table. In her bedroom, his clothes were folded neatly on the chair in the corner. Tears welled up in her eyes as she got ready for bed. She slipped under the covers and curled up around the pillow he always used. She fought back her tears, not wanting to cry over him.

* * * *

She jerked awake and stared up at the ceiling. It had taken longer than normal for her to get to sleep now that William wasn't there to share her bed. She rolled over and closed her eyes. The loose board in her hallway creaked — it only did that when someone stepped on it. She felt her pulse start to race. She knew it wasn't William. He wouldn't have broken his promise to her about staying away from her tonight. A scraping sounded right outside her door.

"William," she whispered, wishing there was some way she could call him for help.

A slight flash of light and William was standing beside her bed. She jerked in surprise at his suddenly arrival in her room. Her gaze shot from him over to where the door was starting to open. She wanted to cry out when a black-clad figure slid into the room. William's hand touched her shoulder for a second before he moved to meet the intruder.

"Thompson, we were wondering where you had gotten to," William said as the lights came on.

Thompson stood blinking in the sudden brightness. She was shocked by the man's appearance. His clothes were ragged and dirty. His hair hung in greasy clumps over his mud-streaked face. There was nothing to remind her of the sleek lounge lizard he had been. His eyes focused on her and she shivered at the intense look of hatred and lust burning in them. Without acknowledging William, the man headed towards her bed.

William reached out to grab the man's arm as he went by. Thompson spun out of the way and turned to hiss at him. Surprise rushed through him, then he narrowed his eyes. William had researched everything there was to know about Thompson and his instincts were telling him this wasn't the millionaire—it was Thompson's body but the spirit inside was a totally different creature.

He started to weave a net from his power. He didn't want Thompson to harm Abby before he could catch him. Tossing the net out, he watched in amazement as the man dodged it.

"Stop." He threw up a wall of power blocking Thompson from her.

Thwarted in his attempt to grab Abby, the man spun around and snarled at William. His eyes turned a deep red and his teeth lengthened to fangs. The creature looking out of Thompson's eyes was not human.

"*Shit. Dominic, I'm in trouble here.*" William threw out a line to the other Enforcer.

"*What's wrong?*" Dominic's voice sounded instantly in his head.

"*I've found Thompson, or more truthfully, he found Abby. I think I know who that true demon was really after.*"

"*Shit is right. I'll be there shortly.*"

"*As quick as you possibly can because I don't think I can take this one on my own.*"

The power emanating from the demon rolled in waves over William. He was lacking full strength because he had been hiding his presence from Abby. The creature leapt at him and he barely had enough time to get out of the way. Its burning breath seared his skin and he smelt the awful stench of its body. He hated fighting true demons because they never understood they couldn't win—he always ended up feeling like he was beating up a stupid animal that didn't know any better.

"Stupid animal might be an apt description of them, but don't forget they are cunning and dangerous in a different way from our brethren. They will try to survive at any cost to them. Our brethren will run before they allow themselves to be hurt in any way."

"Why aren't you here?" Thompson missed his body by inches the second time. The claws transformed the man's hands into lethal weapons. *"This demon is strong enough to change the body he's using."*

"I'm not at full power and I don't want to use what little I do have by transporting myself. I'm only minutes away."

"Those might be minutes I don't have." He felt the sting as one of the claws caught his arm.

"That wasn't good. Make sure it doesn't spread."

He could feel a tingling already starting to move up and down his arm from the wound. True demons had a poison on their claws—it could paralyse him if he didn't take care of it. He took a little bit of his power and created a tourniquet to stop the poison from travelling further. Thompson headed towards him again. William threw out his fist and landed a solid punch to Thompson's stomach. His fetid breath washed over William's face, making him gag.

"She's mine."

"No, she isn't." He slammed another punch to its face. Blood spurted from Thompson's nose and dripped on the floor where it left burn marks. The skin on William's hand started to burn.

He glanced towards the bed to see if Abby was still okay. He felt an anxious jolt when he saw it was empty. Where had she gone? Another swipe of claws caught his attention. He couldn't let her disappearance distract him—he would need all of his wits to keep both of them alive.

Another punch to the head didn't seem to make any difference to the creature. He swung a roundhouse kick to its leg and drove into the kneecap. The leg buckled and the demon lurched. A vase crashed over its head. William felt his eyes widen and his heart jump when Abby appeared behind the demon, the shattered vase in her grip. Weaving, it dashed at the blood running down its face.

It whipped around, reaching out to grab her. William threw his arms around its body, ignoring all the burns caused by the blood. He couldn't let it take her. Dominic appeared in the room and pulled her out of the way, facing the demon. William let it go and moved to Dominic's side, placing their bodies between Abby and the creature.

"I'll not fight the both of you." It pointed a clawed finger at Abby. "The girl is mine and I'll get her someday."

"Over our dead bodies."

"That can be arranged." The demon disappeared in a haze of sulphuric smoke.

William turned to look at Abby. Backed into a corner of the room, she was shivering and her eyes were filled with tears. He took her into his arms and held her tight, trying to make her feel safe. He ignored the twinges of pain as she ran her hands over his arms and up his shoulders to wrap them around his neck.

Dominic allowed them a few moments of comforting each other, then he touched William's shoulder.

"We need to get your wounds taken care of. True demon's blood is almost as deadly to our kind as the poison on their claws."

Dominic led the couple into Abby's kitchen. Earthenware bottles and towels appeared on the table. He gestured for William to take a seat. She sat in the chair next to him, not letting go of his hand. He knew she was scared, but she was handling her fear well. Not many mortals had run-ins with true demons and it could be a terrifying experience. He hissed as Dominic poured some liquid on the burns.

"This is a distilled mixture of belladonna and opium." Dominic touched a damp towel to the large cut on his arm.

"Isn't belladonna deadly?" she asked, not taking her eyes off William's wounds.

"It is to mortals. For reasons I haven't been able to figure out, belladonna is a healing agent for fallen angels. Our cell structure is different, so it might help us break down the poison differently. I'm a herbalist, not a doctor. All I know about any healing comes from trial and error." Dominic continued to wash the cuts.

Abby cringed. "Why don't you just heal yourself like you did me the other night?"

"First, I'm not at full strength. That fight depleted me pretty much to empty. Second, wounds by true demons can't be healed using our power. It was the same when we were angels—maybe God's trying to even the playing field a little bit by giving them this advantage over us." William drew in a breath as Dominic cleaned a particularly deep burn.

"So what was that thing? I know it looked like Thompson, but that wasn't the same man that harassed me."

"It was and it wasn't. When a true demon possesses a mortal, it takes over the body. It will dig into the mortal's mind and find old hatreds or obsessions, like Thompson's for you, and use them to cause pain. So there are pieces of the mortal still left in the body, but mostly it's just the demon running things." William watched as Dominic closed all the bottles then made them disappear.

"What's a true demon?"

He pulled her onto his lap and hugged her close. "A true demon is a creature that has been around as long as there have been angels. The balance of nature demanded that if there were to be beings of ultimate good then there must be some of ultimate evil, so true demons were created as counterparts of angels. Before the Fall, we fought them because it is our nature to abhor evil. After the Fall, there were far more fallen preying on mortals than true demons, so the Enforcers focused on the fallen. We have to, or nature would become unbalanced and destruction would follow. The true demons still cause trouble and we take care of them when we can, but we tend to ignore them if they aren't directly involved in our problems." He looked at Dominic over her head.

"Thank you."

Dominic smiled and nodded. *"You're welcome. Take your woman to bed. I'll keep watch the rest of the night. You need to sleep off the effects of the poison and the belladonna."*

"One of us should notify Mika'il about this."

"I'm sure he already knows, but I'll tell him anyway. It looks better if it seems we are cooperating with him."

"You're right. I'll talk to you later on."

"I'll be here."

He stood up and carried Abby to her bed. William would have to figure out how to deal with the burns in the carpet, but that would be later. He laid her down then covered her up. She grabbed his hands as he started to pull away.

"Don't leave me." Her eyes held fear.

"You didn't want me here to begin with. I won't force myself on you just because you're scared."

She shook her head. "I'll only feel safe if you hold me in your arms while I sleep. I won't blame you in the morning. I need you tonight."

William didn't have the heart to deny her anything. He stripped off his clothes before climbing into bed next to her, then tugged her to his side and tucked her head under his chin. "Go to sleep. I'll be right here all night. Nothing will harm you again." Her sigh held relief. Kissing her hair, he willed her to sleep.

Chapter Ten

William woke up to see Abby staring down at him.

"Hey," he said softly. "How are you?"

"That should be my line." She touched his face.

"I'm used to it, sweetheart. Did you have any nightmares? True demons aren't the most pleasant things. I've only met one that wasn't overtly evil, though I'm not sure what he was truly trying to do in Detroit."

"How did you know I needed you?" She rubbed her thumb over his cheek.

"I had been sitting outside since I followed you home." He put his finger on her lips to stop her protest. "I wasn't going to leave you unprotected. I would have left you alone. You wouldn't even have known I was around if it hadn't been for the demon. You were crazy to think that I would expose you to any danger."

Pulling away from him, Abby sat up then wrapped her arms around her knees. "I can't complain, since you saved me. Thank you."

William slid his hand up and down her back, trying to offer her some comfort. She didn't flinch away from him. "What scared you last night, Abby? Why did you want to get away from me?"

She sighed. "I started worrying about losing myself and becoming your shadow. A relationship with you would be overwhelming and intense."

"I'm sorry. I didn't realise I was being over-protective." He sat up and took her hands in his. "You're so fragile, not because you're female, but because you're mortal. I've lost so many friends and I can't stand the thought of losing you. I don't know if you can understand how much I care about you."

She could hear the pain in his voice. His losses explained the deep sorrow she had always felt in him. "Your watching over me isn't being over-protective. I know that you're keeping me safe. I had a flashback to my childhood. My mother lived for my father — she allowed him to do anything he wanted. I vowed I would never do that."

"I don't want you to let me do whatever I want unless it's in bed." He leered at her and his eyes sparkled with happiness.

He was trying to make her laugh. For a while, she wanted to forget about her worries and just enjoy having him in her life. Smiling, she reached up and wrapped her arms around him. She kissed him while she ran her hands down his sides to tickle him. He jerked then attacked her sides with his nimble fingers.

They wrestled around with the pillows and blankets falling to the floor. Soon she was shrieking and he had her pinned to the bed. He trailed his tongue down her throat to the cleft between her breasts. She bowed her back, offering up her nipples to him. He licked her through her nightgown. The feel of the damp silk against her sensitive skin excited her. Her pussy grew slick with desire.

He left her nipples and moved to her feet. He kissed them and she couldn't help but giggle. He glanced up from the end of the bed and she basked in the glow of his smile. She was surprised when he leapt off the bed and raced out of the room. She heard a crash and then a curse as he ran into something. A thud came from the direction of her kitchen.

He ran back in, holding a red and white can. "I thought I saw this in there."

She helped him strip her gown off then let him push her back against the pillows he had picked up off the floor. She gasped as he squirted whipped cream on her nipples.

"The cream has always been my favourite part of any dessert." He eyed her breasts with a rather fevered glance.

She cried out as William took a long swipe through the cool mounds of whipped cream. She reached out to touch him and he moved away. When he came back holding a pair of her stockings, she shuddered.

With an anxious look on his face, he asked, "Are you okay with this?" At her nod, he chuckled. "Good. I don't want any distractions while I eat." A wicked gleam shone in his eyes.

Abby allowed him to bind her hands to the headboard with the silk around her wrists. They were tight enough to ensure that she couldn't touch him, but she knew they would easily come undone if she tugged hard.

William grunted with satisfaction when he had tied the last knot. "Now you're my captive. I can do as I please with you."

He leant down and brushed a kiss over her lips.

"You do know that what pleases me the most is making you come. I could get off just on the sound of you screaming my name. All you have to do is say stop."

She knew he was waiting for her acknowledgement. Deep in her heart, Abby knew he would never hurt her on purpose. This moment was the point of no return — she was committing herself fully to this fallen angel. She nodded and felt an easing of her fears. Whatever came next, they would face it together.

He looked down at her cream-covered breasts and back up at her with a glint in his eyes.

"You seem to have lost some of your topping, darling." He sprayed more on her then he settled in to feast.

The combination of hot and cool intensified the sparks flaming through her. Soon she was crying out with each suck and nibble. Her moans and his groans mixed to create a symphony of passion.

Lust swelled inside her until she was arching her back and begging him to fuck her. Her juices flowed, making the inside of her thighs slick. He found his place between her legs and never broke contact with her breasts. A single hard quick thrust and they both shouted.

When he could move again, he untied her wrists. She quickly pushed him over onto his back and secured his arms with the same stockings.

"I always wanted to try a cream-covered cock."

His cock proudly jutted out, almost as if it begged for her to taste it. She mounded the white cream on it and over his balls. He grew harder and his sac tightened. He wrapped his hands around the wooden slats of her headboard. He was afraid he would tear the stockings, grab her head and fuck her mouth hard and fast. He didn't want to take control like that—he loved being under her control.

He yelled as she took him into her mouth. Abby licked and swirled her tongue around his length. She nibbled and sucked, taking his shaft as deep into her throat as she could then barely letting the head get past her lips. Abby fondled his sac, then moved to his ass. When she pressed the tip of her finger into his opening, he almost came apart. He could hear his voice pleading with her to fuck him.

Pulling away, Abby smiled at him then straddled his hips to rub her wet pussy against him. He tried to penetrate her but she wouldn't let him. Finally after torturing him for a few more minutes, she took him in her hand and placed his head at her entrance. With one thrust, they came together and they came apart.

He wasn't sure if he had lost consciousness or not, but when he became aware of the world around him, he could feel tears on his cheeks and chest. Abby was lying over him like a blanket. Her face was buried against him and she was sobbing.

Jerking his hands free, he wrapped her tight to him. "Hush, love. It's okay." He stroked her back and arms until she quietened. He rolled them onto their sides. Brushing the tears off her cheeks, he kissed her gently. "What's wrong?"

She laughed shakily. "There's nothing wrong. That was the most intense orgasm I have ever had. I felt like I had left my body and for a moment, I didn't want to come back. I wanted to stay in that place and feel those emotions forever."

He nodded. "I felt the same way." He touched her face with his fingers. "Never in all my centuries of living have I ever experienced that."

William suggested they call Dominic and drive up to Virginia City, wanting to keep her from feeling overwhelmed. He hoped it would help her feel more comfortable spending time with him in public. After Abby agreed, he called Dominic. The other Enforcer didn't mind going sightseeing, so they planned their trip.

* * * *

William stood watching Abby and Dominic cheer on the gunfighting actors in the main street of Virginia City. Her hair sparkled and her eyes shone. Her laughter rang out like a bell. He felt lightness in his heart as if a heavy load had been lifted.

"You love her." It wasn't a question.

He didn't look at Mika'il. "Yes, I do."

"Good. You weren't meant to be alone."

"Why do I feel scared for her then?"

"Well, there is the fact of a true demon stalking her. Once that is cleared up, though, you'll still feel scared because she's mortal and of this Earth. You will always fear for her." Mika'il reached out and gripped his shoulder tightly. "If you embrace that fear, it'll make you strong. Your love for her will free her in so many ways. It'll be like you're helping a butterfly emerge from her self-imposed cocoon. Without you, Abby would never have enjoyed a gunfight in the Old West or a jazz concert in the park. By embracing your fear and your love, you're allowing her to lose her own fears."

William looked up into the eyes of the archangel. In them, he saw the deep loneliness that always seemed to haunt Mika'il like a half remembered dream.

"Tell her."

"I will," he promised.

Another hard squeeze then Mika'il disappeared. William went over to her and put his arm around her waist. Tucking her close to him, he allowed her joy to swamp him.

* * * *

They were sitting on William's couch after a relaxing loving session on his living room floor. She pulled his shirt on and looked at him. There had been something weighing on his mind ever since they had left Virginia City. She figured she would let him work it out and he would tell her in his own time. He hugged her and she felt him take a deep breath and she tensed, waiting to hear what he had to say.

"Abby, do you know how much I love you?"

She jerked back from his chest to look at him in surprise. "How could I know? This is the first time you've ever mentioned love." She felt tightness in her chest. She couldn't believe he was saying the words.

After setting her aside, he stood and walked to the fireplace. He took a photograph off the mantle, then brought it back to her. She stared at the picture of a young blonde woman.

"Her name was Monica. When she died five years ago, I swore never to get involved with another mortal."

"You asked me out."

"Yes, I did when I realised I'd rather risk an eternity of pain than go through one more day without you in my life." He took the picture from her and set it on the coffee table. Wrapping his arms around her, he pulled her onto his lap. She was speechless, having never inspired anyone to risk heartbreak by loving her.

"My father was never around much when I was a kid. He was always gone chasing another crazy scheme. My mom did her best but there wasn't any way she could make enough money to cover my father's debts. I learnt not to rely on anyone but myself. I figured I didn't want to find someone to love. I had only seen the selfish, betraying kind of love and the truth hiding behind a pretty lie." She met his eyes. "Then I yelled at you in a bar and everything changed. I had never met a man who could walk away from a pot and a deck of cards. When I needed you the night that demon attacked me, you were there to protect and support me even after I pushed you away. My father never would have done that."

"You will never be alone again."

"I'm here for you as well, love. I will be yours for as long as I live." She cupped his cheek with her hand.

"That would be forever, if I had my way." William smiled at her.

Linking her hands behind his neck, Abby pulled his mouth to hers. The kiss started gently and calmly, a testament to love and promises. It quickly turned into something hot and explosive. Drawing back, he took a deep breath before coming back for more. He seemed to be drinking from her lips. She played with the hair at his neck, running her fingers through it and enjoying the soft thickness of it.

William caught her face with his hands and tilted it at a better angle so he could get deeper access to her mouth. He thrust his tongue in and out while moving his hands from her face to her hips. He shifted her so she was straddling him without breaking contact with her mouth. With each thrust of his tongue, he ground his erection into the V of her thighs and showed her how much he loved her.

* * * *

Later on, Abby stood, thinking about what William had told her. William loved her. It was still hard to believe that someone as perfect as he was would fall in love with her. She had been so stunned by recent events that she hadn't thought about his story. If she thought William was crazy, she would have to think the same thing of Dominic. Yet after everything they'd gone through the last couple of nights, she really shouldn't be freaking out like this.

Panic made her heart race. Was she a magnet for crazy, obsessive people? What an idiot she'd been to overlook all the comments he had made throughout the days they were together. She must be desperate to just accept everything at face value.

"How is he supposed to prove he's a fallen angel?" A voice came from behind her. "Isn't fighting a demon for you, and appearing out of nowhere enough for you?"

All casino activity had stopped, like someone had pushed the pause button. When she turned around, the same man who had convinced her to go out with William stood before her. He gave her the impression of immense power and enduring timelessness. His silver eyes told her he had seen a massive amount of heartbreak and yet he'd survived.

"There isn't a union card to prove who he is." Sarcasm dripped in his voice.

She shrugged. "Who are you?"

"You may call me Misha, if you wish."

She could tell it made no difference to him what she called him. "How do you know William?"

His stare was like an old soldier reliving his war days. "I've known him since time began. We have been through a lot together."

"So you're a fallen angel as well?"

Misha looked insulted. "Of course not. I would never have followed that lying Daystar."

She took a step back from the rage that burned on his face. "Can all angels stop time?"

He glanced around. "No, only a chosen few can."

"So that makes you a very special angel, Misha?"

"You can think that if you like. What are your problems now with William?"

"Aside from the fact that he believes he's a fallen angel and I don't believe in them, there's the question of his loyalty."

"Loyalty?" Misha looked puzzled.

"If he was an angel and rebelled against God, then he must not have a strong sense of loyalty." Abby shrugged. "I'm not sure I can commit to a man who wouldn't stay loyal and honest to me."

He reached out to grab her shoulders, but she moved a step farther away. "I could just shake the brains out of you, but I'm not sure you have any." At her look of outrage, he sighed. "Sorry, I shouldn't have said that. The fact that William rebelled only proves his impulsiveness, not his lack of loyalty. He regretted it as soon as he was banished."

"Sure, once he was punished, he would be upset. Why didn't he think of the consequences before he did anything?"

Misha smiled. "The best thing about William was always his impulsive nature. He loved to try anything once. He would tease and joke around, but if he knew it hurt someone, he would apologise. He was never cruel. His banishment changed all that. Now, he is cautious and not nearly as much fun." His eyes darkened. "Daystar could charm the leaves off the trees when he wanted to. He is the ultimate deceiver. So I wasn't surprised when they rebelled."

"They were angels. They weren't supposed to turn against God."

He shrugged. "Maybe not, but they should have been given some leniency because of the spell he put over them."

"So instead of leniency, they were turned out of Heaven, stripped of their wings and branded. That's fairness for you."

"Fairness exists in their punishment. He didn't destroy them. He chose to allow them to live here on Earth. He chose to allow them to work for Him still if they wished to." Misha turned his eyes on her and stated, "I didn't come to you to talk about the fallen. I came to tell you that your fears are ungrounded. William can't hurt you. It would destroy him. You are his soulmate, Abigail, and you must find a way to let him into your heart."

"Letting him into my heart isn't the difficult part. Mending my heart after he leaves will be the hardest thing I've ever done."

"He won't leave you. Not on his own. If he has to leave you, please understand that he would have a very good reason to do it. Now that you have connected, his heart won't let him leave." Misha looked disgusted. "I could stand here all day and argue that he loves you and won't leave you, but in the end, it will be an act of faith for you to believe him. Faith in him will help you find his love."

Abby held her ground as he reached out to touch her face. He cupped her cheek in his large hand and stared at her for a moment. She could feel warmth coming from his hand and entering her body. It went to her heart and she felt the chains she had built around it unlock and fall away. Tears filled her eyes when her heart beat for the first time without the constrictions of her past.

"I have freed your heart, Abigail. Now it's your job to find the man who will free your soul." Misha touched his lips to her forehead then disappeared.

She jolted back to herself when the ringing of the slot machines shrilled into her ears. Everyone was playing and laughing like they had been before time had stopped and her life had changed for good. She felt lighter. Staring at the men sitting in front of her, she didn't feel the usual disgust in her heart for them. Instead she felt pity and a sadness that they would never be loved the way she was. They would never love anyone like she loved William.

Chapter Eleven

Bursting from the employee's hallway, she was disappointed to see Dominic waiting for her. She felt her smile dim.

He laughed. "I don't normally cause that reaction in pretty women. I guess you were hoping I was William."

Reaching out, Abby hugged the handsome Enforcer. He looked at her in surprise, like he didn't get hugged very often. He embraced her tentatively. "I won't lie and say that I wasn't really looking forward to seeing William, but you're almost as handsome, so I'm not complaining."

"Good recovery. Well, my instructions are to take you home and leave. No coming and having dinner or anything like that with you. I'm relegated to eating by myself."

Smiling, she followed him to the car. "I'm pretty sure you could find a date if you wanted to."

Shaking his head, he opened the door for her. "There's only one woman I want to take out for dinner and as soon as all this is over with, I'll be heading back to her."

"What's she like?" she asked him when he climbed into the driver's seat.

"She's my best friend and the only woman I could ever trust." The tone of his voice told her he didn't want to talk about the woman.

"Tell me about New Orleans."

Dominic spent the rest of the trip telling her about all the marvellous sights in his hometown. "You'll have to get William to bring you on a visit there once all of this is taken care of," he said as they pulled into her driveway.

He escorted her to the house. William held it open and allowed her to enter. The men shook hands before Dominic left. She turned to watch William shut the door. He kissed her cheek and took the bag with her work clothes in it from her hands.

Pushing her towards her bathroom, he said, "There is a hot bubble bath already drawn for you. Go and relax for a while. Don't worry about dinner. It'll be done when you're ready."

She gasped as she walked into the room. William had filled the tub with water and frothy bubbles. Candles were lit and covering every inch of counter space she had. A vase with a single yellow rose bud sat on the side of the tub. The stereo played jazz throughout the house. She stripped and put her hair up. Stepping into the water, she sighed. The warmth was relaxing muscles she hadn't known were tense. The scent of cinnamon filled her nose and she wondered how William had found out what her favourite smell was. Leaning her head back, she let the soft strains of jazz wash over her. When he touched her shoulder, she opened her eyes halfway.

William stood beside the tub dressed in a deep red linen shirt that was unbuttoned enough to reveal most of his magnificent chest. The shirt tails hung out over the black slacks he wore. He was barefoot and holding a wine glass. Leaning over, he set it down and kissed her lips. He nibbled and sucked at the bottom one until she whimpered. He pulled back slowly and straightened. She eyed the large bulge in his pants and ran her tongue over her lips. He took a deep breath and laughed.

"None of that, love. I want you to relax and if I stay in here any longer, you're going to have a flooded floor and an empty tub."

She tempted him with a husky laugh. "I wouldn't mind."

"Maybe not, but dinner would definitely be burnt if I let you distract me again." He smiled as he adjusted his straining cock. "Take your time, love. I'm going to stuff ice cubes down my pants."

She howled with laughter, imagining the sophisticated William unzipping his pants and pouring buckets of ice down them. "Just don't get frostbite. I would hate for you to lose any sort of feeling there because of me."

"Well, if I freeze it, darling, I know a nice warm place to thaw it in." His voice trailed into the room as he made his way down the hall.

She sipped the nice Chardonnay he had brought her. He appeared again with a plate of Swiss chocolates. She noticed that his erection was still alive and well. He saw her eyeing it and shuddered.

"I couldn't do it. No man would willingly stick his cock in ice." He offered her a chocolate and slid it between her lips.

She swirled her tongue around the offering and his fingertips. Groaning, he withdrew his fingers and grabbed another piece. She let him feed her two more pieces before she called a halt. She knew her pussy was wet not only from the water but from the passion that was swamping her. She sat up in the tub. His eyes went directly to her tight nipples showing through the bubbles. He held out a hand to help her from the tub.

"I would be a gentleman and help you dry off, but I'm afraid once I get my hands on you, I'm taking you to bed and we can forget about eating." He handed her a towel that he had warmed for her. "There's something in your bedroom that I would love for you to wear for dinner."

She took her time drying off. Spreading on the vanilla lotion that she loved, she thought about all the effort he was going to trying to make the evening perfect. The bubble bath, wine and chocolates were wonderful, but it was his willingness to suffer a little to make her feel special that made her eyes fill with tears. She made her way to her room and spied the box on the bed. Her hands trembled as she opened it.

Nestled inside the white tissue paper was an emerald, satin sheath dress. It was accented with cream lace at the plunging neckline and the thigh-high slit. There wasn't any underwear in the box, so Abby knew she was expected to go without, which was fine with her. Her skin was flushed and sensitive—just the rubbing of the satin against her nipples was sending heatwaves through her. Slipping it on, she turned to look at her reflection in the mirror. The dress fitted her like a glove. The lace emphasised her breasts and the length of her legs. She cupped her satin-covered breasts and squeezed slightly. Abby moaned—she couldn't wait for William to touch her. Checking the box again, she found a small jewellery case tucked in the tissue. Her mouth fell open in shock when she saw the multi-faceted, heart-shaped emerald.

She hung it around her neck and read the card.

Abby, if I had a soul to give, it would be yours as well. All I have to offer is my heart. I know you'll keep it safe.
Love, William.

Tears tracked down her cheeks. How could she not love this man? William was trying to prove to her just how much he cherished her by all the sweet things he was doing. She realised his heart would stay behind if he ever had to leave her, and he wouldn't risk that.

Abby left her hair down and went to the dining room. Candlelight bathed the fine crystal wine glasses and china on the table in a soft glow. His eyes lit up when he walked out of the kitchen and saw her standing there. The bulge in his pants was even more pronounced. Holding out a chair for her, he let his hand caress her shoulder briefly as she sat. Pouring her some wine, he didn't take his gaze from her. She could physically feel the trace of his passion as he followed the pendant down into the valley between her breasts. Her nipples peaked beneath the satin. He smiled at her.

After they'd eaten, Abby could only assume that dinner had been wonderful—he had made all her favourites including crème brûlée for dessert. Yet she didn't remember any of the food. She had been too caught up in the love and passion that were flowing from him in waves. When he stood and offered his hand, she was more than ready to join him.

William led her down the hall back to her room. Somehow there were more candles lit and the covers were turned back on her bed. She looked at him in surprise.

"It's magic, darling." He grinned as he stripped off his clothes. "Don't," he said as she started to take off the dress. "I want to make love to you while you're wearing it. I want to compare the feel of your skin to the texture of the satin."

Abby blushed but did as he asked. She knew the first time was going to be quick. Her thighs were slick from her juices and she was more than ready to take his cock inside and let him ride her. He crushed her against him and groaned as the warm satin teasingly caressed his aching cock. William reached down and ground her hips into his. She could feel the wetness of his pre-cum through the material. He lifted her and laid her down on the bed. He crawled on top of her and stroked her with his entire body. The feel of his chest rubbing the silkiness of the satin and lace over her nipples made her cry out. Abby arched her back, trying to get him to move harder and faster. The competing sensations of his hard cock and the soft material over her pussy made her beg. William started circling his hips, making sure that his erection hit her clit every time.

All the muscles in Abby's body tensed when his mouth closed over one of her nipples. The wet satin clung to her as he suckled. She wanted William to take her, but he didn't seem to be getting the clues. He continued to allow the satin to embrace his cock instead of her pussy. When he rotated his hips against her in one particularly hard circle, she came. Crying out his name, she felt the world explode around her.

Her body was still in the throes of her orgasm when he pushed the hem of the dress up and plunged into her. They both yelled as the contractions of her pussy muscles gripped his cock in almost painful waves. One thrust was all it took and he shot his cum into her hot and deep.

"There's no comparison, love," he panted as they both tried to catch their breath.

"What?" She was lucky her brain was functioning enough to ask the question.

"Your skin is much softer than the dress. Now, let's get you out of it. I want to make love without any barriers at all." He stripped her out of the dress and laid her back down, staring at her like he was worshipping at the altar of a goddess. "I love you so much, Abby. You are my whole life."

She reached up and touched the cross on his chest. He shivered as she traced it. "I love you too. I had my doubts, but an interesting man came and chewed me out about them. He made me see that I was meant for you and I'll never let you go."

Tears were welling up in William's eyes. He smiled down at her as she brushed them away. "What was the man's name? I'd like to thank him."

"He said to call him Misha. That was it."

His face registered shock for a moment, then understanding. "I know who he is."

Before she could ask any more questions, he kissed her deep and long. Throughout the night as the candlelight dimmed, the passion flared hot and they bound each other in the fires of love.

Chapter Twelve

Humming, Abby got ready for her shift. She and William had spent all night making love and she was pleasantly sore. They had talked about their future and she had decided to quit her job. She had always hated dealing and the gamblers brought back memories she would like to forget. He had promised her that even if he never placed another bet, he had more than enough money to support them both for the rest of her life. She had handed in her resignation and she just had to get through the next two weeks.

There hadn't been any sign of Thompson and she knew it was worrying William and Dominic. The fallen from New Orleans was proving to be a good friend. He had celebrated their love with a champagne toast and an offer of a vacation in New Orleans. They were planning on taking him up on that after the stalking situation was taken care of.

She wondered who the woman was that Dominic loved. He called her often and would talk to her for hours, but he never mentioned love to the woman. At least not in the conversations Abby had happened to overhear. He had told Abby he didn't want to say anything over the phone when she had asked him why he didn't tell the woman. She figured he was just afraid of rejection and didn't want to mess up a great friendship.

The woman never noticed him standing in the shadows. His red-tinged eyes watched her every move. He knew it was time. She was his and he needed to stake his claim. She had already allowed the fallen to touch her—he could smell the stench of Heaven on her. He checked his watch. He had a while before her shift was over. He would go and set everything up, then come back to grab her. She needed to be purified in death to remove that awful smell. He knew he could never convince her that the fallen were evil. They had always been able to cast spells over mortals and cloud their brains against true demons. He hissed silently. The demon made sure no one noticed him slip into the employees' hallway as he set about planning her abduction.

Abby didn't pay attention to the man in the hallway as she made her way to the employees' room. She was opening the door when an overwhelming smell of death and rot assailed her nose. Before she could cry out, a hand clamped over her mouth and dragged her head back. She felt fear shoot through her. How had Thompson got past all the guards? As she lost consciousness, she prayed that someone would notice him dragging her out of the casino.

* * * *

William looked around the parking garage as he walked to the employees' entrance. There was an uneasiness riding him. Something was going to happen and he was afraid it had to do with Thompson. As he leaned against the wall, he smiled as he remembered the night before. He and Abby hadn't been able to get enough of each other. There were times when he felt so connected to her, he could read her thoughts. He had used that connection to his advantage to make her beg for him. He felt his cock harden with urgent need of a repeat encounter.

Burt burst through the door. He looked around wildly and spotted William. He dashed up to him. "He's got her."

William stiffened and glared at the bartender. "Who's got her?"

"Thompson grabbed her at some point. Probably when she went for her break." Burt held out the emerald necklace William had given to Abby the night before. The gold chain had been broken.

"Damn! I should have stayed with her at all times." He took a deep breath to calm the rage inside him. "Burt, call the police. Let them know that Abby's been taken. How long has she been gone?"

Burt took a step back from the anger in William's voice. "Around an hour or so, I think. I'll let them know, sir."

"Tell them I'm looking for her and will let them know if I find her." William grabbed the necklace and waved Burt back into the casino. *"Dominic, I need your help."*

* * * *

Thompson stared down at Abby with disgust plain on his face. Drawing back his foot, he kicked her in the ribs. She gasped and curled into a foetal position. *Something must be broken.* Her next breath felt like a knife had been driven into her left side. She didn't know how long she had been in Thompson's hands. He must have grabbed her as she was leaving work. It would have been the only time William hadn't been with her.

"William, where are you?" she thought.

"I'm coming, love. Don't do anything to make him mad." William's voice sounded in her head like he was standing beside her.

She wanted to laugh out loud but the pain kept her quiet. *"I think right now my breathing is pissing him off."*

A wave of anger and fear washed over her. *"Are you hurt?"*

"Yes. I don't think I'm going to be able to stay conscious for much longer."

Thompson leaned over and grabbed a handful of her hair. He forced her head up and back at an angle she thought would surely break her neck. He backhanded her with such force that she felt her lip split. He let go of her hair and slammed her face into the floor. She felt her nose break and blood pour down her face. What a way to get a nose job, she thought.

* * * *

William whirled around when he heard Dominic appear next to him. His heart was racing and the fear had dried his throat. He had never been this afraid, not even when he'd been banished from Heaven and had realised the extent of his fall.

"Thompson has her."

Dominic saw the necklace clutched in William's hand and his eyes filled with worry. "I know."

"The one time I can't be with her and he grabs her." William scrubbed his hands through his hair. "Some guardian I turned out to be."

"We both made a mistake. I underestimated the demon's obsession with her. It is as much my fault as yours that she's at his mercy now." Dominic gestured to William's car. "I think we need to find her."

"I don't know if I can." William threw Dominic the keys. He knew he wasn't in any shape to drive. "I made contact with her, but I'm not sure if our bond is strong enough for me to use it to locate her."

"Do you love her?" Dominic pulled out of the parking garage and headed towards the business area of downtown.

William thought of her laughter and her anger. He thought of the moments he had spent making love to her and the moments he had spent just looking at her. He remembered the feeling of joy he got just from hearing her voice. "Yes, I do love her and if I lose her, I just might go crazy."

"Then use your love and find her. Are you at full power?" Dominic glanced over to see him nod. "Of course you are. You've been fucking like bunnies ever since you got her in bed. Concentrate on her. As we get closer to her, the feeling will get stronger. I have an idea where they might be."

William closed his eyes and thought about Abby. He envisioned her looking like she had the first time he'd ever laid eyes on her. A golden glow surrounded the image as he did. It began to intensify the farther into the city they got. By the time Dominic stopped the car, the light was so bright that William could barely discern her in the middle of it. He opened his eyes to find they were parked outside a downtown building.

"Why are we here?"

Dominic climbed out and stood looking up at the windows. "Thompson has offices in here. I figured he would take her some place near to the casino. He doesn't want to be transporting her too far. He feels like you have defiled her and he won't want her anymore."

"If he doesn't want her why did he take her?" He followed Dominic into the building.

"So you can't have her either." Not stopping to check the floor listings, Dominic went straight to the elevators. "Is she here?"

"I believe so. By the time we stopped, the light around her was so bright I couldn't see her anymore." He looked at the Cajun. "How did you know we could do that? Have you done it before?"

"Yes." Dominic's tone warned him that the topic wasn't open for discussion.

"Well, I'm glad you knew it would work. She's on the ninth floor. At least, I get the strongest vibe from that number."

The other Enforcer punched the number and they rode up in silence. William worried that they wouldn't get there in time to save the woman he loved. The doors slid open just as a gunshot sounded.

The two men looked at each other and took off running in the direction of the shot. They burst into the room as Thompson was about to pull the trigger for the second time. There was no way they could reach him in time. Dominic raised his hand and sent power surging into the madman. With a scream, Thompson's face contorted and the demon flashed into appearance. It reached out its claws trying to get a hold of Abby. Dominic's power was enough to overwhelm the man's body so it couldn't move.

The demon swore at William. "You touched her and corrupted her. Abigail was mine until you tempted her to evil." Drool ran from its mouth. It fought the restraints it was under.

William glanced at Dominic, who had to do something or the demon would break free. Focusing his power into a sharp bolt, Dominic shot it into Thompson's body, killing him instantly. The demon screeched as the body housing it collapsed.

"She should have been mine."

Dominic shook his head. "She was never meant to be yours. Leave before I'm forced to kill you."

The demon screamed as it headed towards the window. A path of destruction was left behind it.

William trusted Dominic would deal with Thompson's body. All that mattered was getting to Abby and stopping the blood he saw pooling under her. It was his worst nightmare in the flesh. He understood now why Mika'il had sent those particular dreams to haunt him. He leaned over to staunch it but he was afraid that too much damage had already been done. He used his powers to try to stop the flow. Nothing was working. Tears dripped down his cheeks as he started to pray. He didn't think of the foolishness of his praying to a God who wouldn't acknowledge him. He knew God recognised Abby and would want to help her. He looked up to see Mika'il standing beside him.

"She can't die," William pleaded with Mika'il. "Not this way." The panic was building as he tried to help Abby. "Do something," he snarled at the archangel.

"There is nothing I can do, William. I wish there was."

He glared at him. "What good is being God's archangel when you can't lift one damn finger to help Abby?"

The archangel's silver eyes shone with tears, seeming not to take offence at the anger in William's voice. "I am sorry."

William rose to his feet. He swore violently at the sky. Anger, pain and loss swamped his heart. "Damn you," he yelled. "How dare you do this to her? How dare you take her life? She doesn't deserve this. She deserves to live and love. Abby deserves to know she is loved." Rage flushed his cheeks and made sparks shine in his eyes even as the tears fell. "I'm glad I rebelled. If you can allow such an innocent to die then I'm glad I'm no longer one of yours."

As quickly as the rage had come it left, leaving behind an overwhelming sorrow. Falling to his knees, William buried his face in his blood-soaked hands and sobbed. "Take me instead. I may have no soul, but I have a heart. Let my heart beat in her."

Mika'il reached out and touched his shaking shoulder. "Do you know what you are asking?"

"Yes."

"You will go to Hell, never to touch foot on Earth or in Heaven again. You will suffer forever."

"I will go crazy in this world without her. Celeste and Dominic would have to hunt me down. If I'm in Hell and she's alive, I'll be happy because she's in the world." He touched her pale cheek with a gentle finger. "I don't know if you understand love, Mika'il, but I'll do anything to keep her safe and alive."

"You would spend eternity in Hell for her."

"Yes."

"So be it. A gift given with sincerity should never be thrown away."

He felt Mika'il touch his forehead and he placed the emerald heart on her chest before his world went dark.

* * * *

"Where's William?" Abby demanded for what felt like the hundredth time. She didn't remember much about her ordeal. She knew she had been shot and she had been sure she was going to die, but when she'd regained consciousness, she only had a few bruises. She had spent a few days in the hospital before coming home. Dominic had stayed with her, but he wouldn't answer her questions about Thompson's death or William's disappearance.

Dominic stared at her, and his usual charming smile was gone. He sighed. "I'm not sure, *cherie*. He hasn't been seen since you were attacked."

"He left me." Her voice broke along with her heart.

"I truly don't believe it was as simple as that."

"It wasn't." A new voice entered her living room.

They whirled to see William standing there. Crying out, Abby threw herself into his arms. He wrapped her to him.

William looked at Dominic, who nodded.

"If you have need of me, you know how to get a hold of me." The door shut behind him.

"Where have you been?" Abby asked.

"In Hell. I was in Hell without you."

When she laughed, he realised she didn't understand. He hoped she never did figure out what he had endured so that she could continue living.

"I've been in Hell as well. I love you and without you, the world is a very dull place." She laid her head on his chest.

He felt Mika'il's presence. *"How long have I been gone?"*

"In her world?"

"Yes."

"For a week."

"How is that possible? I feel like centuries have passed."

"Time works differently for God."

He nuzzled Abby's hair. *"Why did He let me come back?"*

Mika'il gave a mental shrug. *"His ways are mysterious. Maybe He believed you learnt your lesson."* The archangel's voice lingered in William's mind as his presence faded. *"I will see you again."*

"Thank you." He sent a feeling of gratitude to Mika'il.

William crushed his lips to Abby's. A moan surfaced as she rocked her hips against him. His cock hardened painfully and he knew he had to have her. Trailing kisses down her neck, he stripped her. "It's been so long, sweetheart. I love you. I need you."

She cried out as his fingers drove into her pussy. She pushed herself against his hand. "William, please," she begged.

He ripped open his jeans. His cock sprang free, urgently seeking her. Lifting her, he wrapped her legs around his waist. He took her with one thrust of his hips. They both cried out as the passion overwhelmed them. Their climax shot sparks through their bodies. For one moment, they were connected — one body, one heart, one soul.

"I'll never leave you again, Abigail Hanson. You are my love and my life," he pledged as he carried her to the bedroom. They both lay down on the bed and he gently touched a finger to the heart in between her breasts. "I'm glad to see you took care of my heart for me."

She snuggled close to him and fell asleep while William watched the scars fading on his body.

About the Author

I've been writing for most of my life, but was first published in 2004. I believe everyone deserves love in all its forms. I write about women and men who find strength in loving each other. I live in the Midwest with my two cats, and when I'm not writing (which isn't very often) I read and watch movies.

Tiffany Aaron loves to hear from readers. You can find her contact information, website details and author profile page at http://www.totallybound.com.

Totally Bound Publishing